Mind-Sprung
A.D. Harvey

What may not be expected in a country of eternal light?
(Mary Shelley, *Frankenstein*)

I went to the woods because I wished to live deliberately .... and not, when I came to die, discover that I had not lived.
(Henry Thoreau, *Walden*)

E o gram Soltão Badur dizia a Martim Affonso Sousa .... que quando de noite queria yr a Portugal e ao Brasil, e à Turquia, e à Arabia, e à Persia, não fazia mais que comer um pouco de bangue.
(Garcia de Orta, *Coloquios dos simples e drogas da India*)

Contents

	Introductory Note.	5
1	TÄRENDÖ	6
II	GÄLLIVARE	16
III	THE APPRENTICESHIP OF EDDY WILLIS	19
IV	SELLING THE PAST	34
V	DOPE	45
VI	MOVING TIME	54
VII	FOREIGN PARTS	64
VIII	SOMETHING ABOUT THE HISTORY OF DOPE	76
IX	FEAR AND LOATHING IN THE FIFTH REICH	91
X	HALF WAY TO THE NORTH POLE	96
XI	LAKATRÄSK	102
XII	WINTER IN NORRBOTTEN	107
XIII	NORRBOTTEN	113
XIV	GOING NATIVE	117
XV	THE RED HOUSE BY THE LAKE	123
XVI	THE TRADE	133
XVII	RETURN TO THE BIG CITY	139
XVIII	A MAN FROM THE PAST	145
XIX	GOODBYE ALBERT	150
XX	END	158

Copyright © 2015 Mandrake & A D Harvey

All rights reserved. No part of this work may be reproduced or utilized in any form by any means electronic or mechanical, including *xerography*, *photocopying*, *microfilm*, and *recording*, or by any information storage system without permission in writing from the publishers.

Published by
Mandrake of Oxford
PO Box 250
OXFORD
OX1 1AP (UK)

Introductory Note.

I wrote *Mind-Sprung* in the spring of 1980 and it is now inevitably something of a period piece. For this reason I have left Chapter XVI, on the illicit importation of hashish, as it was originally written. During the last three decades the growing trade in heroin and cocaine, which weight for weight are far more valuable than hashish, has marginalized importation of hashish; as far as I can tell nearly all the dope nowadays smoked in Britain, whether old-style grass or newer-styled skunk, is grown here in indoor cannabis farms using artificial light, and hashish in the form of blocks of green or brown resin, which used to be the staple in Europe, is now apparently very rare. But all that is another story. Chapter VIII, on the history of hashish, bhang etc., has been somewhat expanded and there is also some additional material in Chapters V and XI. Elsewhere I have merely corrected typographical and verbal errors and very occasionally altered phrasing. The book was originally published under the pseudonym Michael Lindsay, mainly because at that stage of my life, having published two well-reviewed academic monographs and seven articles in scholarly journals during the previous three years, I was still hoping to establish myself as a respectable scholar.

A. D. Harvey   Stoke Newington, May 2014

Chapter 1

TÄRENDÖ

The surface of the earth was over-run with ugly little creatures who stood on their back legs; most of them wore cow-leather and rubber coverings to protect their hind feet. They killed or captured all the other animals they encountered. They had developed crude medicines to protect their own lives to such an extent that most of them were able to continue alive long after they had become damaged or ailing; consequently they appeared a race of cripples and invalids. They lived in large groups in warrens built on the surface of the earth. Their dominant characteristic was an obsession with mechanical tasks, which were perhaps useful for their group survival but of which they had forgotten the precise purpose. They had a mania for organizing things in ever more complicated ways. They excited themselves with complex but meaningless fantasies, especially on the subject of the relationships they had with one another, and they rotted their minds and bodies with over-indulgence in drugs, such as alcohol and hashish. Some of them even wrote books.

This is a book.

During the late 1960s and early 1970s a large number of books were published about dope — cannabis, pot, marijuana, hashish, bhang, ganja, let's call it *dope*. Because of the nature of their subject these books had a superficially international flavour, but they were mostly

American and reflected American attitudes to dope. It was very much the prosy amateur academicism of the American middle class which imprinted itself on the solidifying image of dope.

The books all peddled the same information, mentioned the same names — Charles Baudelaire, Théophile Gautier, Allen Ginsberg. And they nearly all give the impression of having been written from the outside. In some cases the accounts of the subjective effects of dope are culled from writings over a hundred years old — Baudelaire — or from descriptions published by members of pre-war literary coteries who tried dope a couple of times and didn't like it. This was taking the American respect for the written text a little bit too far.

Other books were more up to date, but in trying to be objective merely succeeded in being tiresome and dull. Perhaps many of the writers were users themselves, but dope can't make someone into what he isn't, only help him move towards what he truly is, and these writers, stoned or straight, were reefer-party pontificators, aware, liberal, concerned, Mr Average-upper-income-group-American bores. Living in the most paranoid country in the world, they shied away from the subtleties of paranoia which dope can offer. Living in one of the most extravagantly beautiful countries in the world, they buried their sense of wonder beneath rubbish heaps of banality and platitude. Living in the most disillusioned decades of their nation's history, they used dope as both a protest and a refuge. It was never really an end in itself. Some Americans, entrepreneurs from the Land God Gave to Entrepreneurs, made money by starting up businesses selling pipes, chillums and other smoking accessories. Others settled down to their portable typewriters and started tapping out their dope-books. They found dope easier to handle as a way of making a living than as a way of life. Or perhaps it was just that the real whole-hoggers had quickly moved on to heroin and died of ODs or blood-poisoning in the bathrooms of cheap rooming-houses in Middle America, or from the gun barrels of downtown hustlers who thought they were Jimmy Cagney: or else had been put away in clinics.

This book is different from all those other books. The writer tried to come to terms with the fact that smoking dope isn't something you do, it's something you are, just as much as using heroin is. But whereas heroin destroys you, dope changes you. Change can be destructive, and the western world is full of over-enthusiastic amateurs who overdid the dope scene of a couple of years and then drew back, terrified at the prospect of becoming different from other people, at the prospect of never getting the safe jobs, mortgages and Ford Cortinas they had been pretending they didn't want.

But there are others who kept following their noses. They know that dope has changed them, and don't resent the possibility that they might still be changing. Perhaps they are the real heirs of yesterday's *Conquistadores* and empire builders. In our smaller, more red-taped world only the voyages of the spirit are still completely free, and what some seventeenth-century stay-at-home said, "We carry with us the wonders we seek without us: there is all Africa and her prodigies in us," is now much truer than when he said it. And yet even the voyages of the spirit might have a physical and geographical dimension. With dope it is still possible to move from the auction show-rooms of London's West End to a lonely road in the Arctic, beyond the northern shore of the Gulf of Bothnia, on a long hot summer afternoon, driving past endless trees and rocks and sky, with an airline bag on the seat beside one, and inside it a Husqvarna *Pistol m/40* guaranteed to function at sub-zero temperatures, though this Arctic summer day it is well above 25°C in the shade.

The most brilliant idea of Eddy Willis's life came to him that afternoon he tried to rob the bank at Tärendö: it came to him at the filling station near Kaukonen, when the two Finnish policemen came across to his car to tell him that they had just heard on the radio that the King of Norway was dead.

"*Kungen av Norge är död*," he said to himself, and he suddenly thought: "What am I doing here, in the Finnish Arctic, having just failed to rob a bank in Sweden, and being mistaken for a Norwegian? After all, I'm *English*."

He thought:

"I am English. I will return to London. I still know lots of people there. The Customs would never dream of anybody being so mad as to smuggle drugs from Sweden to England. I shall be the first person in history to smuggle something from a country where it is expensive to a country where it is cheaper."

He had accumulated a huge cache of top-quality homegrown grass, raised from the best seed. He would be able to unload £10,000 worth in a single trip to London; in Sweden he knew only a small dealer in Skellefteå, who couldn't possibly have handled so much. And drug-smuggling was bound to be less strain on the nerves than bank-robbery.

The idea of robbing the bank in Tärendö had been his one desperate attempt at earning a living in Sweden. For a few moments, as he drove along Route 397 towards Tärendö in the Volvo he had stolen in Norway, with a surging mind-fuck of Wagner's March of the Valkyries blaring out on the cassette player — he had slipped the cassette into his pocket just before he had left home, counting on the off-chance of there being a player in the car he stole — for those few moments on his way to rob the bank at Tärendö, he had felt that he was actually doing something real, for the first time in years. Perhaps the first time ever. He had left Gällivare some way behind, and had passed the last of the huge surrealistically modern iron-works shimmering in the heat haze like Martian invaders amongst the spruce-clad hills. These iron-works were there to remind you that this Back of Beyond was World League. The sheer size of the country gave the massings of trees and the sweeps of the hill-slopes a kind of symphonic structure, tantalizingly out of step with the rhythms of the Wagner on the cassette player, yet so beautiful too in the bright sunshine, for all that there was a vast featurelessness about it, a kind of all-embracing anonymousness in which he felt he could hide.

Hide. He had been hiding for years, from nothing, from phantoms, from imagined figures from his past who stalked him amongst the fir trees. And now at last he was going to have something *real* to hide from; for to commit a crime on his own doorstep, armed robbery no less, was to make a final commitment to this strange country where he had dwelt for seven years. It was a kind of sacrament even. He had been an outsider for too long, for all his Swedish wife and Swedish kids. His identity had been his dwindling bundle of Dutch guilders which had kept him going for seven years in barren independence. But now he was going to become a real Swede, a front page story in the *NSD* and other provincial newspapers.

There is no finer feeling in life than to be bowling along at 100 km per hour in a stolen car, with a 9 mm Husqvarna *Pistol m/40* concealed in an old airline bag on the seat beside one. The *m/40* looks like a Luger, though with numerous improvements, including a switch which enables one to empty the whole magazine in a single burst, like a machine-gun. It was said that the Swedes regarded premeditated crime as typically Anglo-Saxon, and certainly, for those few moments, he felt very happy with the prospect of becoming a real live bank-robber.

The first hint of the town he was about to rape were the telephone wires on poles converging from different directions across the wastelands, then a junction with another road, and lots of blue and white signs quivering in the heat — 13 km to go. He passed a lake, with huts for tourists dotted on its further shore; more huts on the fringe of a wood; a sign saying "Turist Inform 1 km." He passed the first farms — he was close to the northernmost farms in the whole world here — and the 110 km speed limit sign, which he would be ignoring on his way out. Apart from a glimpse of small blonde children outside one of the farms, the township seemed deserted, poignantly calm, this victim he was about to pillage. But he enjoyed feeling guilty, it was like salt, giving an edge to flavour. Of course they said in Sweden that robbers should be free to carry on the profession of their choice, same as anybody else. It would mean a system of State Insurance against the depredations of men like himself, but such a State Insurance scheme would be cheaper than all these nice shiny new prisons. It was bound to come soon, the Swedes were bound to be the first nation to take the fun out of crime; but right now he was enjoying the feeling of violation.

The 90 km speed limit sign was opposite the wooden church, grey-walled, green-steepled, and then came the first town houses, and then the Kalix River, with the bridges for which Tärendö was famous all over Norrbotten — one of them a huge through-arch bridge with a fifty foot high arch, they must have enjoyed building such a monster in the middle of nowhere. He turned left at the next junction. A couple of parked cars by the road; a teenage boy. He passed the Savings Bank and did a 360° turn round the little square. It was a big country and the people were spread thin; communities like this one seemed miniaturized. There was a small *Konsum* (consumer co-operative supermarket) with a small *Hotell* on the first floor; and opposite them the small fire station, the small post depot, the small *Folkhus*. It was the original Swedish version of Sleepy Hollow. The clothes shop next to the bank, though open, had nothing on display in the window. There was no such thing as impulse-buying in these backwoods, so there was no need for advertising or sales promotion.

He parked in front of the bank. The next house beyond was of wood, painted Falun red in the traditional style, but the bank was of loud orange brick, like a villa in a housing estate in the English Home Counties. Half of the building was occupied by a flower shop, the other half by the bank, his destined victim, open 1400-1600 Mondays, Wednesdays and Fridays.

The teenaged boy had gone into the *Konsum*. Eddy leaned sideways over the passenger seat beside him, transferring the pistol from airline bag to inside pocket. He got out of the car. Even in this apology for a town-centre, the hot silence of the Arctic summer was almost a shout. He pushed open the door of the bank. There was already a customer, an elderly woman. The bank was a single neat room, four metres square, divided into two by an open-fronted counter topped by an illuminated sign saying KASSA. It occurred to him at this, the last moment, that the reason there was no security grill was that the bank was too small to be worth robbing.

The old lady turned away from the counter. Her faded eyes had that hint of craziness in them that was one of the features about the older natives. She scarcely glanced at Eddy; people who ignore even their neighbours do not take much notice of strangers. Eddy held the door for her.

"*Tack, tack.*" Thanks very much. She was gone.

He stepped across to the bovine blonde behind the counter, his hand reaching inside his jacket to grasp his — cheque book?

"*Hej, älskling!* " Hello darling. The door burst open, and all at once the room was full of policemen shouting greetings. There was only two of them, but it was a small room. They were tall and pale and moved with a self-conscious swagger, like well-fed State Troopers in an American movie, like knights of the Arctic wildernesses. They spoke to the cashier in Bondska — I suppose the term might be translated *Peasantish*, i.e. rural dialect — and Eddy could just about make out that they were on their way to Masugnsbyn and had stopped by to say hello.

"Let me serve this gentleman first," said the girl turning to Eddy.

"I left my cheque book in the car," Eddy apologized. He squeezed past the two policemen. With their automatic pistols and truncheons they seemed almost too bulky to get past.

His legs felt so weak, he nearly fell over on the doorstep. Ten seconds later he would have been standing like an idiot with a gun in his hand and two armed policemen round his neck. Or, if he had been a few minutes ahead of schedule, he would have run into the police in their car on the road to Pajala.

The whole beauty of his scheme had been that in this huge, empty country, there were not many police, not many witnesses, and just enough roads for there to be too many to road-block; and there was a convenient foreign border just beyond Pajala. But the main element in his plan was surprise; he had counted on the police not knowing what to do. After hitting the bank he had planned to drive north on Route 397 till he reached Route 395. If anyone has seen his Norwegian number plates they would count on him heading north-west, either to Kiruna, where he could abandon the car and catch a train to Narvik in Norway, or else to head across the mountains to Tromsø. From Pajala the first available police car would be sent to the scene of the crime, possibly they would also send a car to reinforce the border post beyond Pajala, and they might even send a car to Muodoslompolo; but in the first twenty minutes after his attack, he was sure they would not block the bridge over the Torne River at Autio, just 8 km before Pajala. Consequently, he would be able to dodge the police, reach the border post from the opposite direction from the bank robbery (driving on private roads which he had already reconnoitred) and escape to Finland before they had even realized they had lost him.

It was no good now. By the time the two policemen were safe out of the way at Masugnsbyn, the bank would have closed. And for all he knew the Swedish police had been notified about the theft of a blue Volvo at Mosjoen, in Norway, the day before. His elaborate scheme had, basically, cocked up. There was nothing for it but to dump the car and get home.

It was, consequently, one very disgruntled English immigrant who was driving along E78 in Finnish Lappland about an hour later, when he was overtaken by a Finnish *Poliisi* car. It was a decayed Saab, and the two officers inside were dour, dark-haired men, in seedy uniforms and sunglasses, smoking self-rolled cigarettes. They didn't have the Hollywood cowboy effeteness of the police in Tärendö; the Finns were provincial — they even thought Stockholm was sophisticated — but they were the toughest bunch of people in Europe, and the *Poliisi*, though they might look like run-down ticket collectors, were tough enough to hold their own. These two passed Eddy quite slowly, looking at him out of blank sunglassed eyes, and for a moment he thought they were going to stop him and harass him about his tyres of whatever — not that their own vehicle was fit to drive. But they passed on, and it was not till half an hour later, when he had stopped at a petrol station hemmed in against the road by fir trees – the dominant species in these parts — and looking like a gasoline station anywhere in the back woods of a hundred Hollywood movies — it was only when he stopped at this petrol station that the *Poliisi* reappeared. They drew up on the other side of the sun-baked forecourt and got out. Again the blank sunglassed faces turned in his direction. They came across to his car and one of them stooped beside his window and addressed him in *Finländare* Swedish.

"We just heard on the radio. The King of Norway has died."

"The King of Norway?"

"We thought you might like to know."

"*Justa. Tack så mycket.*" Of course. Thanks so much. He was not sure how much grief or distress your average Norwegian would exhibit on hearing that the ageing Olav V had snuffed it, but he succeeded in looking thoughtful.

He drove on, heading east, deeper into the endless forests which stretched beneath the blazing sun far into the Russian Federation.

The odd thing was, though he managed to tune into a Norwegian radio station — Narvik or Tromsø probably — the crisply gabbled news bulletins mentioned nothing about King Olav.

Just after midnight he dumped the car in a small lake near Posio, rolling it off a ledge into the deepest part of the waters. It was still daylight, though no birds were singing and a terrifying hush held the woods which closed in all around him. Then he set off to walk to the main road where he would be able to catch an early morning bus to Rovaniemi.

From Rovaniemi he would be able to catch a train home.

And after home, he had decided, the next step would be London.

Chapter II
GÄLLIVARE

The train reached Gällivare half an hour late. In the immense unpopulated spaces of the far north they didn't worry so much about efficiency and punctuality as they did in the cities of the midlands. Perhaps the hazard-free summers were too brief for people to readjust after the annual seven months of snow-drifts, avalanches and ice.

In spite of the train being behind schedule, there was a handful of people waiting patiently outside the old-fashioned wooden station-house. The only good-looking woman amongst them was his wife Barbro. Beside her, coming up to her waist, were the two flaxen-haired Aliens, talking together with serious, concentrated faces. As he crossed the tracks from the platform where the train had stopped, Eva called out "*Hej!*" and they left their mother's side to sprint towards him. He stopped and took them in his arms. He heard a double click from behind them; that was his wife taking the mandatory family snap-shots.

"Have you been in Stockholm?" asked four-year-old Lars.

"Is Stockholm a long way away?" asked five-year-old Eva.

"You *know* it's a long way away," said Barbro, as if saying it for the third or fourth time. "I showed it to you on the map." She picked up his airline bag, leaving him with both hands free for the Aliens. He found that he was unable to avoid glancing nervously at the bag, to make sure, for the *n*th time, that it was properly zipped-up, as if there was a risk she would glance inside and find the inexplicable, inexcusable pistol; her father had given it to him, but that was no reason for him to be taking it to Stockholm in his luggage.

They walked to their car, which was parked round the other side of the station. Against the back-drop of neat characterless offices and shops, their Volvo was beginning to look distinctly old and shabby. This made Eddy feel guilty. It didn't do to stand out as too different, didn't do to have too old and shabby a car.

The characterlessness of Gällivare, the pure under-stated austerity and impersonality of this materialistic civilization on the outer frontiers of the universe, never ceased to have a poignant freshness for him. The sameness of the buildings seemed an index of the sameness of the people's psyches; he sometimes felt that in Sweden he was relating to only one composite individual, of whom his placid aloof wife and well-adjusted kids were only a component. And he felt impelled to share this sameness. He wanted to seem exactly like everyone else, even down to the age and appearance of his car; it would be a kind of disguise, like these children of his, who looked so much like archetypal Swedish children, especially Eva with her pig-tails.

The Aliens climbed into the back seat of the Volvo.

"Is Stockholm a long way away?" Eva asked again, as he got in in front of them.

"I'll show it to you on the map when we get home," he said.

"We have been to the library," Eva said. She showed him a book of black and white photos depicting the various stages of pregnancy and childbirth.

He wondered how he was going to tell them he would have to leave them again, this time for at least a month.

He had been thinking in English for at least the last twenty-four hours. English, a shapeless, spineless, ambiguous, muddy language, full of suggestions and cross-connections and possibilities, had fitted in with the new world of possibilities he had discovered in Finland. Perhaps it was an old world rediscovered. It was an effort to switch back to the clean, mincing, unimaginative sterilities of Swedish. A whole dimension in his perceptions filtered out when he switched from English to Swedish.

"I'm going to have to go away again soon. But for much longer this time. I have some business to do in London."

"Then we'll come too," said Barbro.

"No," he said.

She said:—

"You've never taken me to England. I've never been to England, and I've always wanted to go. I thought when I met you that you would take me there. I feel very dull here. Living here is not always so interesting."

He said:—

"It's impossible. This is very important business, I can't afford anything to go wrong." But already he could see that there would be advantages in having them along; a husband and wife and two small kids would have no trouble at the Customs.

"*Vi vill komma.*" said Eva from the back seat. We want to come.

And so it was that Eddy Willis decided to take his whole family on his smuggling trip to London.

But you're probably wondering what he was doing in Sweden in the first place. Let's step out of sequence, go back a few years, fill in some details.

Chapter III
THE APPRENTICESHIP OF EDDY WILLIS

He came from Samesville, one of those little Ealing Comedy towns in southern England, which are each innumerably the same, each sprawled around its well-preserved but rarely-entered medieval church, the proof and emblem of its uniqueness.

He was one of those tens of thousands who were cheated by being born into a Britain on the very eve of its sudden ignominious eclipse and loss of Imperial Mission. He grew up with world maps coloured one third red, to become a citizen of a country that had lost its purpose.

He stuck out Grammar School right up until the Sixth Form:— the *please sir* this and the *yes sir* that, the ugly purple uniforms, the standing up and sitting down in unison, the no running here and the no talking there, the insistent drone of propaganda — the house, the school, the way we do things here, the well-tried traditions. Sometimes, in the dank corridors with the echoing bells and shuffling footfalls, he wondered if he had been sentenced to death, to living death; his punishment for passing the eleven-plus to be years in dreary penal institutions followed by decades as a lobotomized cabbage in an office.

In the Sixth Form things became a little better. They could stay in their class-room during break, and play pontoon or rummy. There was even a set who thought themselves exceptionally grown-up and sophisticated and played contract bridge. Prefects no longer shouted *"Quiet there!"* in Assembly — in fact Eddy nearly became a prefect himself — and very self-consciously one or two of the teachers tried to enter into an embarrassed man-to-man, colonel-to-subaltern intimacy. But this slight amelioration merely underlined how pointless staying on was.

It was 1966 and the Swinging Sixties were starting to swing: but not where he was. He got a week-end job humping crates in an off-licence. One of the other people there, a lad of about twenty, suggested they should go to Guernsey together to pick tomatoes. This new acquaintance, Terry, was quite good-looking, a bit of a Rocker. He had left school at fifteen. If anything, Eddy despised him for not having gone to Grammar School, but on this one matter of going to Guernsey he seemed to have had the right idea and Eddy didn't mean to allow his prejudices — his parents' prejudices — to stand in his way.

Guernsey wasn't as much fun as predicted. Terry and he found work on a fruit farm easily enough, but they were sacked in a couple of days. There were problems finding somewhere to stay, and sleeping on the beach caused backache. Then Terry got himself a girl, a skinny little thing with a black leather mini-skirt and grazes on her knees, and a stammer. He had been going steady with a girl back home, continued to speak of her frequently, telephoned her occasionally. The new girl was just, you know, a bunk up, but her intrusion gave Eddy his cue to split from Terry, and after only a couple of weeks he was standing on the outskirts of Winchester, trying to hitch a lift to London.

London. He knew it only as a confusion of vast headache-giving buildings, and the view of endless terraces from the window of a railway carriage. He had not even any clear physical notion of what sort of place he might find to live in; he even assumed most Londoners lived in quite big apartment blocks, just round the corner from Oxford Street. But he knew there were lots of things going on in London, if only he could find them, lots of girls, and interesting places to hang out, and all the emptiness of his past short life might be filled. The Friend who was going to be on exactly the same wavelength as himself, whom he had theorized about in 4C, but never found, was sure to be already living in London, in some obscure garret, only waiting to be encountered by chance across a billiard table in the smoke-filled back-room of a pub, or on a street corner in Notting Hill when the Queen went past.

He found a job as a warehouseman, held it down for just under four months. Then he thought he would learn a skill, and got a job in an antique restoring outfit in Camden Town owned by a big ginger-haired cockney wide-boy named Albert. Because he was the youngest there Eddy was practically the tea-boy, but soon, when Albert fired the drunk who operated the tank of caustic used for stripping paint, he was promoted to chief stripper. Mainly it was doors, chairs, kitchen tables: – heavy stuff, especially some of the Georgian front doors, which left him knackered at the end of each day but built up his shoulders. The Friend didn't manifest himself and most evenings he went out drinking with his work-mates, went to a couple of West End discos, hung around Kensington looking at the snazzy boutiques, met a girl in a pub whom he touched up confusedly in a doorway round the corner from Goodge St. underground station. He even tried the Round House but it was too full of hippies.

He liked London. He liked the polychronic garishness, the unconvincingness of its cement and plate-glass lushness. He liked the skyscrapers that had sprung up everywhere, distant and incongruous but as perfect in their detail of windows and aerials as if they had been giant toys in the next street. He liked the jet-liners, alien invaders with their gem-like splendour, slowly banking above the acres of shabby terraces, and the sky sunset-pink at midnight, and the ozone whiff off nipple-punctuated T-shirt fronts, swaying bums like scaled-up peaches, pub forecourt sunlight glinting on the sheen of small hairs on the tanned forearms of other blokes' girls. But still he seemed to be waiting for something to happen.

On his eighteenth birthday a man who occasionally drifted into the workshop to buy half a dozen second-hand doors said he could use a "big strong lad." From what he said, the work somehow involved "niggers". It didn't sound too interesting, but the man mentioned there might be a room for him along with the job, and the place Eddy was staying, in Cricklewood, just a room with a family, was noisy, inconvenient to travel to, and he didn't like the people.

"Take it," said Albert, the boss of the antiques outfit. "You're too young to settle here, though you'll always be very welcome back."

The first day of the new job consisted of stripping loathsomely rotted wallpaper off the walls of an apparently derelict house near Paddington Station, and pulling up old lino and burning it in the back yard. He enjoyed the burning — lots of black oily smoke. George, his new employer, came by with another man to examine the floors, to see if they needed replacing, otherwise he spent the day alone.

The following morning, George came to the house shortly after Eddy had started work. He said:—

"We've to evict some geezer and his wife what are behind with the rent. Ever done anything like that before? You'll be coming along with Sam and me. Don't expect any trouble, just a bit of shouting."

They arranged to meet up at George's office at 11 a.m. After an hour of wallpaper-stripping, Eddy strolled round to the office. He hung around there for half an hour. The secretary, a pleasant woman in her late thirties, was very vague as to when George was likely to appear. People drifted in and out, looking for George. To each of them she would say, "*Eddy's* seen him, so he must be around somewhere," and they would look at Eddy and say, "Where was he, then?" Eddy thought of going off to the caff down the road for a second breakfast, but it was a new job and he didn't want to begin by skiving. George turned up at last, accompanied by a man in his late twenties with LOVE and HATE tattooed across his knuckles.

"This is Sam," said George. "Watch how he does it. He's one of the best in the business."

Sam was carrying a cricket bag, very greasy and battered, and excessively weighted down at one end by something inside it.

They drove in George's Rover to Notting Hill. The houses, white stuccoed, with steps up to pillared porticos, bay windows and, in some cases, balconies, looked like chic guest houses at a smart seaside resort — or would have done if they had not been so astonishingly filthy and decayed. Washing hung on lines between rusting drain-pipes; coloured children played beside a lamp-post. As they got out of the car, a West

Indian woman, who had been standing at a front door, retreated into her house, slamming the door behind her. The three of them walked down the pavement a little way. George found a key on the large key ring he was carrying and let them into a house. In the hallway the smell of desolation and damp made Eddy wonder if the building had not been standing empty and derelict for years. There was no wallpaper, no lino. In places large patches of plaster had come off the walls and ceilings, showing the mildewed laths beneath. Half the banister was missing. Keeping to the disintegrating wall, they climbed to the second floor and stopped in front of a door. George kicked the lower panels three times.

"You in there, Briggs?" he shouted.

"Fuck off man, leave us alone," said the voice within, a black man's baritone.

"Your rent's overdue. You're evicted. I want you out."

"What rent, you fucking bloodsucker? Nobody don't pay that much rent for a hole like this one. You fuck off now, you frightening my kids."

"Lazy fucking nig-nog, why can't he get a job and be out at work when we call round?" said Sam in a semi-undertone to Eddy.

George banged on the door with his hand, testing how many places it was bolted in.

"Two bolts and I guess the lock," he said, "Bolts about here and here." He pointed to two feet above and two feet below the keyhole.

Sam opened his cricket bag and took out a sledge-hammer, some pieces of oak board, and some sticky tape. While George shouted through the keyhole at his tenant, Sam fixed pieces of board with the tape over the places where he meant to hit.

"Not a bad door, see," he pointed out to Eddy. "No sense in smashing it up too much, cost maybe two nicker to get another to fit. Also, if someone calls the Old Bill, there's no smashed up door to point to."

He hit the door with the sledge-hammer five times, not even swinging very much, though each blow seemed to concuss the whole house. At the fifth blow, the door burst open. In the tiny, stinking room within were a smallish West Indian and his woman, each of them holding a baby.

"That's it, Briggs," said George. "You're evicted. Or do you want us to jump up and down on you a few times before we let you go?"

"Hey man, why you doing this to us?" said the black man, dancing uncertainly from one foot to another, and dribbling slightly with fear, or anger. "I aint got no place to go to man, and I got two kids too, where they going to sleep if you throw we out?"

"Why don't you just fuck off back to the jungle where you came from?" said George.

The whole business took six minutes. Eddy then spent a couple of days clearing up the place, cleaning the walls preparatory to repapering them. Occasionally he could hear the other tenants scuttling out of sight on the stairs. George called in a couple of times and walked around saying, "This'll be real nice when we've smartened it up. A spot of fresh paint will make all the difference. People'll pay five, six pounds a week for a room here, once we've got it into shape." But eventually, it seemed, he sold it as it was to another small property company.

During the next six months, Eddy must have been involved in over thirty evictions. Sometimes, when it was old age pensioners who were to be evicted, it would be just Sam and himself. "Old people is

OK," Sam told him in the pub one day. "Pensioners, you can do anything with them. Piss in their flower pots. Take all their trousers out of the wardrobe and chuck 'em out of the window. You know, humiliate them. That's the best way. Mate o' mine says to this old geezer, 'Take out your teef.' Old geezer takes 'em out, matey grabs 'em, throws 'em on the floor and stamps on them. Crunch. Very satisfying that. An' what's the old geezer suppose to do, go to the police and say to the desk sergeant, 'Sergeant, some bastard stamped on me falsh teesh?' No way. Moved out the same day, he did." But usually there were four or five of them, because they would be evicting West Indians who would get violent, and sometimes might get a couple of their friends round to help them hold out, so there was always a good chance of a punch-up. Sam got his head kicked in one morning. "I don't mind," he said. "I'm used to it." But he had to be laid off evicting for a couple of weeks, until his black eyes healed, because it was asking for trouble, throwing your weight around while bearing the signs of having been stomped. So Eddy graduated to the sledge-hammer. His new side-kick turned out to be a rather poncey bloke in his early thirties who used to terrify their victims (clients?) with learned quotations. "While worldly men are justly said *through fear of death to be all their lifetime subject to bondage*, to the righteous only it belongs to look on death and smile." To Eddy he confided, "Blind them with philosophy, that's the way to do it. Man, they really hate philosophy." Another of his gimmicks was, when evicting old men, to interrogate them on their politics:—

"Did you vote Labour in 1945?"

"Don't know. Don't remember."

"Cos if you did, it's thanks to cunts like you we have a Welfare

State. You know what a Welfare State means? It means there's homes for human rubbish like you what is too old to take care of themselves."

Naturally Eddy didn't want to appear less tough than his mates. They spent a whole week going on a round of preliminary heavying of pensioners whom George planned to evict within the next month or two (some of them were paying fixed rents dating from the early 1950s) One of the pensioners they visited had a canary in a cage, rather a scruffy, unhygienic, pallid specimen. Eddy reached into the cage for it, before the pensioner could even protest, and bit its head off. It tasted revolting. He spat out the spiky, fluffy, shit-tasting head on to the carpet, vowing never again to try the same trick, but he knew he was on the way to establishing some kind of legendary reputation for himself.

And this would, as often as not, be going on just around the corner from the trendy Portobello Road, and after a successful mission they would mingle with the crowds around the antique stalls, ogling the female tourists or looking over the latest clothes in the boutiques.

Once or twice George said to Eddy, "There's more to the property business than running about like a New York gangster, kicking around geriatrics and third-rate niggers. Property means hard work." And he would set Eddy to painting skirting boards or laying lino. But Eddy never finished these jobs, nor knew if anyone else finished them either, because he would be needed for his main business as an evicter. The work amused him and though he wasn't paid very regularly, he only had to ask George for "a sub" for the latter to hand over a couple of fivers without a word. He reckoned he averaged twenty pound a week — good money in the 1960s — for doing very little, sitting around in cafés – he got to know all the backstreet workingmen's caffs north of the river — chatting up girls and doing the occasional business visit.

Then one day he smashed open a door and five West Indians came out fighting. Eddy got one of the blacks in the goolies with the butt of his sledge-hammer, and managed to reach the front door. He didn't wait to see what happened to the two men who were his companions that day. (They were eventually thrown out into the street, each with broken arms, but he only heard about that later.) He left the sledge-hammer — by now a favourite — wrapped in a *Daily Telegraph* in a luggage locker in Paddington Station, and spent the day in Richmond Park. In the afternoon he picked up a blonde art-student named Debbie in Crust's Caff, up the road from the Odeon in Richmond town centre. When he phoned George that evening he discovered that he had been right to lay low; the police had been round to ask questions, and though nobody was being charged, George was being warned to clean up his act — i.e. no more heavy stuff.

Eddy was still not yet nineteen, but looked older, partly because he had grown a moustache, partly because he was so heavily built. His career in "property" had toughened him, but he was ready for a change. He had enjoyed the atmosphere of violence; the reality of violence he could handle though he saw no future in it, and congratulated himself on having known when to run away. He had had no moral compunction about what he was doing. He used to say, both then and later, "Of course I'm anti-social. In this world, either you're anti-social or you're kicked around like a football." He used to quote a Moroccan proverb he had picked up: "If you are a peg, endure the knocking; if you are a mallet, strike."

All the same there had been many aspects of George's operation which he had disliked. Too often he had listened while George enthused about his plans for some property — it would always be a more than averagely shabby one, too — only to find out that within the week George had sold it at a bare profit in order to settle some pressing debt, or worse still, to find money for "a very special investment." And too often he had turned up for a rendezvous previous to an eviction, only to be kept waiting endlessly, his stomach churning with tension and from pacing up and down. He knew that George was essentially "an amateur", with much more appetite for money than talent for grabbing it. Amongst the talents needed for grabbing money, Eddy always thought punctuality and adherence to planning ought to be pretty high on the list. And there were all sorts of ways he saw in which George's operation could be tidied up, for example, giving tenants several warnings, then not going near them for a month, then watching to see when they left the house and breaking in to throw out their furniture and belongings and to fit padlocks. He didn't like to suggest this, in case people thought he was afraid of the personal confrontations — which in reality he enjoyed — but it did seem a more efficient method. But basically Eddy objected to the pettiness and shabbiness of George's whole operation, and guessed that it wasn't likely to be long before the police began to put George out of business. There was talk of neighbourhood groups trying to organize against illegal evictions; talk of complaints to local councillors, or even to Members of Parliament; and what Eddy took more seriously, talk too of West Indian gangs planning to fire-bomb George's properties, perhaps even fire-bomb George if they could find him. It was one thing to say, "Stupid fucking coons, they couldn't hit the sea if they pissed over the side of a boat," while flinging some West Indian's pathetic belongings out of an attic window; it would be quite something else to say the same thing when drenched in blazing petrol mixed with sugar. In fact it all seemed too much trouble for something Eddy didn't at all believe in, and so he decided to try something new.

He had a couple of drinks with Sam, who spoke eloquently about debt-collecting. "Basically, low-grade heaviness. So-and-so owes money for some deal. 'Okay, we'll put the frighteners on him.' Matey turns up at his front door, rings the bell. Mrs Unpaid-debt opens the door, don't matter if it's on a chain, matey shows her the front end of the sawn-off shotgun he's got under his anorak. Into the sitting-room. There's Mr Unpaid-debt sitting at his ease in the sofa, watching telly, perhaps a couple of light ales within reach. Matey tells Mrs Unpaid-debt to sit down beside her old man. One way to do it is to make 'em sit on the floor with their feet on the sofa — makes 'em feel ridiculous, makes 'em feel at a disadvantage, and they're not so likely to try anything, though basically if you're at all worried about the customers trying anything, this business aint for you. So there they are, them on the sofa, matey with the sawn-off shotgun. Two barrels, see. He fires one barrel into the TV. Got any idea what a mess firing a shotgun at a telly makes? Bang — whoomf, both together. Good idea to be wearing sunglasses. Bits of TV screen fucking everywhere. You couldn't say what'll bother 'em most, paying for a new telly or picking up all those little tiny pieces of razor-sharp glass. And you've still got one barrel left in case they think of getting stroppy. So matey reminds 'em they're owing money and that's it, he let's himself out. Going rate for that kind of job's fifty quid. Not bad eh? And it's worth it to the bloke who hires you, you can bet your fucking life the debt gets paid pretty sharpish after that."

"Ever do a job like that?" Eddy asked.

"Known people who have," Sam said, and he began talking about the time he had been thinking of working for the Krays. But Eddy knew he was just bullshitting; evicting blacks and stealing the odd spastics' collection box from outside a chemist's (using bolt-cutters to break the security chain) was about the limit of Sam's personal experience.

In the end Eddy became a driver for Oxfam. He had become a connoisseur, a real expert, of the belt of mid-Victorian housing that stretched from Notting Hill Gate up to the Harrow Road, from Kilburn in the east to Acton in the west. George had occasionally talked to him quite freely about business, and he could guess the market value of any house in any street in this area. More than that, he could sense the ethnic identity of any area from the smallest clues, judge the atmosphere of any pub merely from the quality of its paintwork — not that he hadn't been in most, and didn't need to guess. He knew which mews were not cul-de-sacs, he knew which caffs did toast and dripping. Perhaps it was the sense of there being so many other areas of London that he didn't know at all that suggested to him the idea of becoming a driver.

He took the job with Oxfam because he guessed the poor money would be compensated for by a do-as-you-like atmosphere and a chance of lifting the best of the second-hand gear they handled. At any rate, it would do as experience while he was looking about for something better. He drove all around, collecting left-overs from church jumble sales, throw-outs from rich people in Hampstead who phoned up out of the blue, particularly obnoxious items like sideboards from long-winded OAPs in Tufnell Park. He furnished a flat quite nicely from his journeying back and forth. Debbie, the art-student he had met in Richmond, pretended to be tempted by the idea of moving into this flat with him, and he shagged her a couple of times on the genuine lambs-wool carpet which he had diverted on the way to the shop from its donor in Swiss Cottage. But in the end she explained that she wanted to be independent, and soon after that they broke up. Well, he thought, women are like buses, there's always another one along in a minute — usually full. But he missed the uneasy symbiosis of sex, and ripping off things from Oxfam, though amusing, was scarcely a substitute.

Once or twice he was asked to take away pairs of kitchen chairs which seemed quite old, or a Pembroke table, or a mahogany chest of drawers. Once there was even a pair of oak hall chairs, ugly uncomfortable things but real antiques, and another time there was a battered davenport. With items like these he would drive round to Albert, the big ginger-haired cockney antique-dealer he had used to work for in Camden Town, and do a deal with him. Often they would end up spending the evening together. Albert was eleven or twelve years older than Eddy and had not paid much individual attention to him back in the days when Eddy had been merely the young jerk stripping doors, but now Eddy was emerging as a source of worthwhile antiques, Albert began to take more notice of him. Fresh from talking about Biafra, or the problems of the Third World, or how it absolutely wasn't true that only ten per cent of donations to Oxfam reached their destination, Eddy would hang around the Camden Town workshop, listening attentively while Albert instructed him. "It's a traditional type of kitchen chair, but they made a lot for the army in the First World War — here, you can see the broad arrow stamped underneath. There's two ways of telling whether a circular table is genuine. One is, as the wood dries out, it shrinks across the grain, so it ends up a bit narrower than it is long. The other thing is, after decades of being moved around, a genuinely old table will always have a ring of dark greasiness just under the rim, from people's fingertips, from the way they put their hands under the rim when they moved it. A genuine Chippendale mirror like this is a godsend. To qualify officially as an antique things only have to be one quarter genuine, so we can cut this frame in four and fit the pieces into four mirrors I'm having carved now." Despite the difference in their age they got on so well together that often they would return to Albert's flat to smoke dope. "Nothing nicer than turning your brain into soup after a hard day," Albert would say.

Soon after Eddy gave up driving for Oxfam and began working for Albert full-time, and not just as a delivery driver either. They went to Phillips together to check out the gear that was up for auction, and it would be Eddy who would be the one who returned on the day of the actual auction, to do the bidding. After a couple of months, Albert stopped going to Phillips with him and left it to his own sole judgment to decide what was worth bidding for. Eddy began selling too, and helped Albert make up his accounts — not that much of the business wasn't transacted in cash, but they needed something to show the Inland Revenue. By the end of 1968 Eddy was a fully fledged antique-dealer accustomed to going around with wads of grimy ten pound notes in his pocket. He had found a career.

Chapter IV
SELLING THE PAST

Albert ran his business from a mews in Camden Town. He had two of the garages as workshops and one of the flats overhead as an office. He lived in another of the flats, which was crammed with the overflow of the workshop: brass bedsteads, kitchen tables, mahogany chairs, an old juke box, filthy, musty curtains heaped in corners, a vast ancient gas stove. People used to say it looked like a room in an old-fashioned workingman's cottage. In the toilet was a roughly scrawled notice saying, "Will gentlemen please help to keep the toilet clean by pissing on lumps of shit stuck above the waterline. Thank you." Though he was screwing a woman in St. John's Wood, Albert lived alone, and after a few weeks Eddy moved in with him.

A couple of the occupants of the other flats in the mews worked regularly for Albert as sub-contractors and some of the others were employed as chippies in the workshop. They formed a happy doped-out community. There was Peter, who was built like a gorilla, with thumbs like big toes. He had been a drummer in a rock group. There was Chris, another of those dropped-out student types who seemed to crop up all over the inner city. "I'm not quite sure I really like doing this sort of thing," he would confide while engaged on some especially filthy job, ripping out decayed upholstery or whatever. He used to talk about a pet scheme he had for writing English Literature dissertations for students in Germany, Austria, Switzerland and the Netherlands, at £300 a dissertation — "the most bizarre international conspiracy of the century" she called it. There was Ivor, whose mind had been burnt out by all the LSD he had taken – but then, every true community needed to have its Village Idiot. There was Kevin, the enthusiast for squatters' rights, always going on about his long struggle against eviction by Camden Council, the poncey officials, the misrepresentations, the thousands spent on the Reform School kids from the Council tower blocks: "OK, it's not their fault they're hooligans, I'd be a hooligan if I'd grown up in one of those vertical zoos, but why the fuck don't they pull all them tower blocks down and build decent houses for people to be decent in, instead of wasting money trying to buy off the hooligans with youth centres and poncey homosexual liberal youth workers, and trying to stop us squatters because we've got more sense than to try to bring up our kids in tower blocks. There's no upper class and lower class any more: the them and the us is the bureaucrats, and the people who just want to live their own lives. I'm telling you, if it wasn't for the fact that all the National Front people I know look like child-molesters, I'd vote for them." There was Dick the driver: "Here we go again, the hand brake's fucked, the indicators don't work, the windscreen wipers have fallen off or something, and I feel like death warmed up. I've had some speed and some sulphate, but basically, all I'd really like to do is drop dead." And over them all, Albert reigned as king. King of the Cockneys, perhaps.

In spite of his barrow-boy accent, Albert was only a fake cockney. Originally he came from Tunbridge Wells. All the same, he liked to give the impression to customers that he was from the East End. Visitors to the workshops were encouraged to believe they were visiting an old-fashioned, perhaps even old-established, firm of artisans — very traditional, a little bit nineteenth-century even, but *very* reliable. They would have been startled by Albert's remarks about them after they left: "Fucking Golders Green Jew — too much money, no sense and less taste." "What a pansy, wouldn't surprise me if he started out in life as a rent-boy." The overall effect of sterling Victorian seediness was slightly spoilt by Albert's newish-looking Peugeot, but this was doubtless construed as typical of the traditional flashiness of the East End businessman. This same out-of-place Peugeot was transformed into the stylish limousine of Albert and his trusty lieutenant when, changed into conservative and only slightly dingy suits, they visited prospective victims to check out how little they could offer for that week's bargains. Apart from their ragged, dirt-engrained fingernails and the patina of toil over their fingers, the pair of them looked exactly like the smoothies people expected antique dealers to be. Albert would be knowledgeable and could bullshit on about court cabinets and Sheraton and Art Nouveau for hours. Eddy, as Trusty Lieutenant, was less communicative, but would pass the occasional friendly comment about hitherto unnoticed defects in the items for sale, so the price could be brought down. They were both good-mannered without being deferential, with no indication of any vulgar another-sucker-bites-the-dust mentality. But as far as Eddy was concerned, it was only make-pretend.

The reality – if there was any reality in this chameleon-like operation – was to be seen only in private, in Albert's flat or, more occasionally, in the flat of one of his employees, when they would loll on a miscellany of battered almost-antique chairs around a vast pine kitchen table, with a bottle of Glenmorangie malt whisky and at least two joints circulating. Sometimes there would be cocaine, even occasionally some opium though Albert strongly disapproved of opium. "That's a drug for women," he would say, "and for all those wretched effeminate skinny men who deal in it." There would be an open fire, fuelled with wood scrap from the workshops, though sometimes in winter it was necessary to make a sortie down the street to find a builders' skip with wood in it to nick, or even to take an old door out of the store and smash it up in the street. A couple of men had electric guitars — Albert had a harp which he couldn't play, though he tried — Pete had his drums — and there were also bongo drums, harmonicas, a concertina. And no neighbours close enough to make objections. Stoned, you perceive more, and more vividly, you are overwhelmed by all the perceptions rushing in on you, as if the filters normally protecting your senses have been taken down; Eddy found some of these musical/ drunken/ stoned evenings almost unbearably enthralling. Round eleven-thirty, when some of the men began to drift back to their women in the other flats, the residue would pile into Albert's Peugeot and they would go for a cruise up Adelaide Road and Haverstock Hill. If they overtook a car driven by anyone who looked timid or, better still, by a woman, Albert would drive close alongside, wind down his window, and shout across obscenities. He enjoyed that. Somehow or other they never encountered the police. Or else they would stroll up to Primrose Hill and stand on the top, looking out over the sea of lit-up buildings which stretched southward to the horizon, with the unending distant traffic rumble like the sound of distant battle, or the audio-ghost of the Blitz. Back in the mews, late at night, Eddy would often stand outside for half an hour, counting the stars, and, before he went in, marking the street as his own with his minute-long widdle.

Eddy was happy in this life. Though he found Albert's employees no more than pleasant enough, the truth was that he considered Albert the most fascinating person he had ever met. He had been beginning to feel that he had been cheated. The vivid social scene he had expected to grow up into had forever eluded him. He had been forced to conclude that he had been deceived as to the likelihood of meeting really interesting people in London, until, at last, Albert came along. A big, freckly-faced man, with a crew cut and strangely pale but seductive eyes, Albert wasn't quite what he had in mind, but that didn't seem to matter. Of course Albert was a charlatan, and knew it, but he was also a man who made things happen. In him the creativity of a Shakespeare or a Michelangelo had been chanelled into small-time entrepreneurship. Buying and selling was not money, it was a kind of Performance art, not to be judged by end-products, any more than a fire is to be judged by its ashes, but by the exhilaration generated at the moment. Not that Albert was exhilarating in any obvious sense, he was not especially ebullient or oppressively high-spirited. Generally he was quiet, confident, enormously relaxed. He was especially confident, especially relaxed, when he was glibly assuring some punter that such and such a job could be done by such and such a date; he positively delighted in the catastrophic delays he inflicted on his customers. And yet even his most disgruntled customers seemed to find he added a new dimension to life, so that everything around him seemed more vibrant, more exciting.

When alone with Eddy, driving to a meeting with a client, or over a bachelor supper in the mews flat, he would hold forth. Sometimes it was simply information about the Real London. "That's the Great Northern Hotel," he would say as they drove past King's Cross. "They do a nice kipper there, good place to go for breakfast on Sundays. No eleven o'clock starts there, it'll be all gone if you're not there by ten." Or passing a shop with its windows covered by posters in a street consisting otherwise only of deserted warehouses, he would break out, "See that place? Best place in London for cheap clobber." Sometimes it was Business Philosophy. "It's not just buying and selling. It's creation. It's perhaps the most creative thing a man can do. It's the art form of money, like poetry is the art form of words, or sculpture the art form of heavy materials. Business is making things happen. Politics is also making things happen, but in politics you have to stick to the system. There's no system in business, you invent it as you go along. You see potential where nobody else saw potential. Like the guys in Denmark who salvaged all these old stoves. You see potential in people too, a possible customer in every man you meet. It's not just a matter of *Hey, mush, wanna buy this?* You have to see what he needs and why, get into his head, see him the way he sees himself, give him a bit of your imagination. But it's no good having the thing here and the customer there, you've got to bring the two together. Business is moving things. Organization. That's where the real flair comes in. Organization is people. You have to see the potential of the people you employ, get them to do things they didn't know they were capable of. And you have to see the potential in situations, too. Any situation, whether it's a skip with a half-way decent pine kitchen table in it with only three legs, or a bloke supping a quiet pint in a pub with a lorry he's driven down from Peterborough parked outside — just driven down this morning and unloaded, means to make his way back at his own speed in time to clock off at four-thirty this afternoon. Offer him a tenner and he'll help you load up and deliver a pile of gear to Hammersmith for you, he'd just as soon earn a tenner for free with his boss's lorry, as sit over the same pint of beer from one o'clock till closing time. Being a businessman is making things happen that wouldn't have happened without you. It's the little people, the little entrepreneurs who're the real creators. They – we – fill in the spaces left between the big, clumsy, inefficient corporations. That's why governments don't like us. Governments like people who pay their taxes and insurance and who can be regulated and controlled, people who see things the way governments see them, in terms of systems and regulations and institutions. But that's not the way I see things. All I want from government is to be left alone."

Eddy said:—

"I suppose we're anarchists if we don't believe in government."

"Anarchists? Aren't they the people who used to go around chucking bombs? That isn't such a bad idea."

So they went to an Anarchist meeting Eddy saw advertised in *Time Out.* They should have known there would be something wrong with it, just from the fact that it had been advertised in *Time Out.* After sitting in a gloomy silence for an hour, listening to the proceedings, they left, taking with them a couple of bent-wood chairs that had been standing in the entrance hall. "They sounded exactly like the fucking Labour Party," Albert remarked. Eddy, feeling guilty at having suggested the visit in the first place, said nothing.

Sometimes, when in a flood-tide of bitterness against government regulation, Albert seemed to see himself as a leader of an underground revolutionary army, one of the leaders thrust to the fore by a raging British population. Soon they would rise up and throw off the shackles of an effete bureaucracy that had castrated itself with the irrelevancy of its own concepts. One could imagine Albert, standing on a street-barricade in a heroic pose, saying things like, "The only way to end unemployment is to abolish nationalized industry before it abolishes us."

He told Eddy one day, "I really mean to go into politics later on.

But to be any good in politics, you need money, lots of money. One day I'm going to make lots of it, and then I'll really show those snotty-nosed wankers something."

After Eddy had been with Albert a couple of years, the longed-for opportunity to make lots of money finally came their way. The Church of England, no less. Quite by chance Albert got to know the Redundant Furnishings Officer of the Diocese of London. As London's population moved out of the inner city into the suburbs and the overspill estates on the further fringes of the Home Counties, many churches had to be closed as redundant. Some were turned over to alternative uses, others were demolished. In either case the contents — pews, altars, lecterns – were disposed of by the Redundant Furnishings Officer of the Diocese. If the church was demolished, the organ, the stained-glass windows and the carved wooden sanctuary screens were disposed of as well. For a period it was possible to buy the contents of an entire church for less than £1,000. But then, with more and more antique-dealers scrambling for a share of the loot, the price began to go up. It was a kind of business that lots of dealers took a sniff at, but most of them didn't stick with it for long. The gear was dirt cheap to buy, but not always so easy to sell. There were few customers for fifty-foot long pews, for brass altar rails, for twenty-foot high stained-glass windows depicting the crucifixion in the worst agonies of Pre-Raphaelite kitsch.

But the worst problem was diocesan bumbledum. Customers were often a pain in the neck, but customers came and went, you never had to bear with them for too long. Business associates were often dilatory and inefficient, but if they were excessively so, you dealt with someone else.

Dealing with the church introduced whole new dimensions of

inescapable harassment. You might be instructed in January to plan the clearance of a church, moving in at the end of February. Absolute must to have the church empty ready for the demolition contractors by mid-March. You would have to run around and line up customers for all the best items; and then still be waiting in *November* to be told when the next committee meeting was to be held that might make the decision that would enable the clearance to go ahead, bearing in mind that the demolition contractors were very impatient and wouldn't allow much time for the preliminary removals. No good complaining though, that would merely be the cue for the official to launch into a two hour spiel about all *his* difficulties in his office. Another thing: certain items had to be taken away, but not sold. Altars, for example, and fonts were on no account to be sold. The Diocese expected the dealers to store them indefinitely. But frequently the Diocesan Redundant Furnishings Officer would hint coyly, "Between you and me, you can lose that altar." Then it would be sold. A week later he would phone up in a panic to say the Archdeacon of What-not had asked about that particular altar — was it still safe in store? Well of course it wasn't, and there'd be a big flap. What with the delays and the eight unnecessary phone calls a day rescinding the previous day's phone calls, most dealers gave up after a few months. That was why there was little serious competition to a take over by Albert of the church gear business in London north of the Thames. Temperamentally Albert was perfectly suited to this style of doing business. He had no sense of punctuality and did not expect it from other people. And he loved talking about nothing on the telephone.

Eddy hated the coy phone calls from Diocesan House, but other aspects of the church stripping business were sheer joy. He liked vicars, for some reason, and the elderly ladies in hats who hung round churches doing the flowers. They made him feel like an alien invader, in his dirty bomber-jacket and bedraggled cord trousers; made him feel part of a civilization that had refined culture-clash away from the crudities of geography, so that he was a latter-day Viking pillaging, not East Anglia, but the older generation in the next street. And he liked churches too. When he went to check out a new church lost in some dreary ganglion of suburban streets which somehow suggested quiet corners of old market towns, Lewes or King's Lynn, he felt good. London was so vast that whole families settled there for generations had never visited certain streets, or even suburbs, but Eddy belonged to a generation of restless mobility, he was one of the connecting principles, and he enjoyed zooming from one suburban ghost town to another. He liked the rubbish-strewn back streets, the ruined privet hedges smelling of semen, the youth gang daubs on the walls — "Even the deaf have heard of Ricky the Skinhead." The church he would be visiting would usually have been standing locked up and empty for a couple of years. It would look depressed and dispiriting and he would have the sense of being about to bring it back to life again. He was going to wave his magic antique-dealer's wand and convert musty old junk into cries of delight from satisfied customers and gratifying wads of used ten pound notes. Glancing with happy anticipation up at broken windows and crumbling stonework, he would insert the key into the keyhole of the great wooden doors with as much breathless eagerness and apprehension as when inserting his willy for the first time into the vagina of a new girlfriend. Every time he struggled with the unfamiliarity of a new door it was a new adventure. Then he would be inside counting the pews — soon, like Samson smiting the Uncircumcised, he would be walking up and down these rows of pews, shattering them with a judicious sledge-hammer, reducing them to easily loaded planking — assessing the quality of the stained glass, lifting up the eagle lectern out of sheer pleasure at the weight of its solid brass, examining the choir screens, which would be getting a good price as decor for a new wine bar, checking out the damp and mouldy carpets in the leaky vestry, counting the processional staffs and the verdigris-darkened candlesticks in corners of cupboards made of pine scumbled to look like oak, pocketing the best of the unused altar candles, glancing at the tawdry prints and mouldering hymn-books and the models made by long-dispersed Sunday School classes, bursting open the poor-box with a wrecking bar, to reveal one or two greenish pre-decimal pennies, and finally climbing up the tower, up ladders inches deep in feathers and fluff and birdshit and the skeletons of long-dead pigeons, to check out the tower clock and, more important, to gaze out in triumph over the surrounding roofs of the community whose temple he had invaded.

Sometimes, driving through Notting Hill, Eddy would think what a long way he had come since his evicting days. He really couldn't imagine how he had made a living like that. It was so crude. And the dope he was smoking seemed to have taken away his taste for violence. Though one could still respond to emergencies, dope seemed to surround the idea of violence and exertion with such complexities of possible consequences that sometimes he hardly dared open his mail in the morning for fear of what he might commit himself to.

But there's more to dope than that of course; which brings us conveniently to the subject of our next chapter.

Chapter V
DOPE

Antique-dealing was only half of his life. The other half was the noisy gatherings in the mews flat, visits to the Camden Plaza and the Hampstead Classic with a quick pipeful of dope beforehand to lend tone and poignancy to the film, the doped-out strolls over Primrose Hill to look at the miniskirted young accountants' wives exercising their red setters, the delicious paranoia of lonely explorations through lush evening suburbs which seethed and throbbed in time to the heavy chords reverberating inside his head, and the unbelievably beautiful sex when so stoned it was all but impossible to concentrate enough to get an erection. Probably he was as much part of the late 1960s scene as anyone else, but his bit of it was a bit that never got into the Colour Supplements. He was in London during the great Grosvenor Square demonstrations against the Vietnam War, but he took no account of that. He didn't even see the Rolling Stones in Hyde Park. All the same, he did smoke a lot of dope.

Perhaps he was a typical dope-smoker. It is difficult to say. Different social groups behave differently, and ideas about which social groups are typical of society as a whole are imperceptibly changing all the time. And when a new and secret custom establishes itself which is admired for its daring novelty but which cannot be discussed publicly because of the constant threat of police interference, each group involved must necessarily imagine that it is the typical and characteristic group.

Because illegal, dope was often regarded as a symbol of rebellion, and because in the late 1960s rebellion was equated with students, there was a tendency to see dope as a student habit. Students may have had a small effect on speeding up the spread of dope — more, one imagines than army personnel, a group of comparable age and geographic mobility — but in reality students were following fashion, not leading it. Some people even claimed that dope-smoking was a specifically middle-class vice — alcohol and later amphetamines were identified as the authentic working-class drugs. In retrospect it can be seen that there was a certain temporary enthusiasm for dope amongst the middle class, and this was manifest amongst the younger middle class at university. But the middle class, for all their underlying Toryism, are the most changeable of social classes. They appear as the leaders of society, not because they are the most constructive but because they are the most responsive to new developments. *Circa* 1968-1972, when a degree of deviant self-indulgence harmonized with the *Zeitgeist*, dope made progress. But the middle class soon began conforming to other norms and the tide turned. According to an article Eddy once read, in 1970 thirty-five per cent of first year students at Middlesex Polytechnic had some experience of drugs, whereas by 1978 only twenty-eight per cent of first years had any experience. By 1980 it was obvious that dope smokers were not, characteristically, the professional representatives of middle-class opinion, academics, local government officers, business executives, television producers, journalists. Members of these professions do smoke, but in isolation, and they can't be said to form a sub-culture. The real dope sub-culture in Britain is on the borderline between middle class and working class. The true heirs of the 1960s are not the middle-class Marxists who led the march on Grosvenor Square; they are the self-made entrepreneurs with hand-to-mouth businesses, independent-minded maintenance mechanics, dealers in fourth-rate antiques, rank-and-file members of the Black Economy, heirs not merely to the 1960s but to the artisan traditions of Victorian England, heirs even to the psalm-singing gendarmerie of Cromwell's New Model Army, and further back, to the barbarian invaders against whom King Arthur fought, who despite their reputation were as willing to till the soil and herd cattle as they were to rape and pillage.

Today these people live in the interstices of Britain's crumbling industrial society. Economically they are the rank and file of the non-unionized parts of the service sector and, proportionately, they are most numerous in the prosperous commuter towns of the south – Colchester, Guildford, Dorking, Chelmsford, Aylesbury, Reading, with outposts out west, in Cheltenham and Bath, and northwards, in Ilkley and Bolton. They are proportionately less numerous in London, but the vast concentration of people in the metropolis means that in terms of actual numbers they are most densely concentrated there. In London too, the tens of thousands of West Indians, amongst whom dope-smoking is established on a different and stronger pattern, and the existence of the headquarters of the dope smuggling trade, means that London is the Mecca of British dope. In some parts of London people even smoke joints openly in cinemas. But just as there is no such person as a typical Londoner, so there is no such person as a typical London dope-smoker. The real professionals amongst the smokers are presumably the dealers. Eddy bought from several in his time: Nick, relaxed, bearded, genial, a bit like a bank manager, always insisting he didn't *like* being a dealer; Annette, who lived on the ninth floor of a council tower block, and had dark bags under her eyes, always name-dropping, always paranoid; Lynn, beautiful, ashen-faced, always talking about the men who were trying to hustle her, always giving short weights; Pete the Pole, good-looking, deferential, facile, unreliable, what Eddy's parents (and eventually Eddy himself) would call an all time *weak character*. But you could no more generalize about dealers than about smokers as a whole. Perhaps the average smoker is a man living in a small flat, or perhaps a squat, who goes out once or twice a week to a pub, usually a different one each time, for he is never completely at home in pubs, having a preference for stark functional drinking places resembling stables, for he is a man who carried his personality around with him and dislikes seeing personality given concrete form — but there's no point going on with this, it doesn't sound in the least convincing.

Though it may be impossible to generalize about the average dope-smoker, other than perhaps to locate him on that middle-class-working-class borderline, it is possible to generalize about the *effects* of dope, though of course this has been denied too.

Dope comes from hemp, the same plant whose fibres are used to make rope. In cool climates, hemp yields plenty of fibre but very little of the drug tetrahydrocannabinol — to give the pharmaceutical name for the active ingredient of dope — and in hot climates, plenty of the drug, but not so much of the fibre. Seed of a drug-yielding strain from a hot area will revert to producing fibrous plants after a couple of years in a cooler climate, and seed from a fibre-yielding strain will produce dope plants after a few years in a hot climate. The female plants yield more dope than the male.

The traditional Indian terms for the various forms in which dope is marketed — *bhang*, a paste, made from the crushed top leaves and flowers, *ganja* the lower leaves, *churrus*, the resin which the plant exudes — are of little relevance in Britain. Actually the terms *ganja* and *bhang* are often used interchangeably, being originally the same thing in different languages; *ganja* is Hindi, *bhang* Persian (the official and court language of India in the seventeenth and eighteenth centuries) and Urdu. *Bhang* — i.e. the paste from the upper leaves and flowers — and genuine pure *churrus* are never seen in Britain, and the grass, or bush, that is sold in Britain is not *ganja* in any usual Indian sense, for it normally contains stalks and seeds.

Apart from grass, the two commonest forms of dope in Britain are both known as "resin" or "shit", being incorrectly thought to be identical in composition, and distinguished only by their colour and presumed country of origin. Green "shit" comes from Morocco where it is known as *kif*. It is made by drying the whole plant, crumbling it into powder, sieving the powder to remove the stalks and pressing the powder into bricks, sometimes with the help of steaming. It is in fact equivalent to grass. Lebanese "resin", prepared in the same way, is often stronger but is more likely to be adulterated. Black "resin" from Pakistan, Afghanistan and, allegedly, Nepal, is quite different. Its active ingredient is *churrus*, which in its pure form is a brittle and shiny resin resembling varnish. This is mixed with lamp black, sugar, sheep dung, henna, clarified butter, vegetable oil and so forth, in order to make it go further. Because the original *churrus* is much more powerful than *kif* or grass, the resulting black muck is as strong as Moroccan, but its effect is much more physical, much less speedy and cerebral. This is because when smoking it one is not smoking only cannabis, one is also smoking sugar, sheep dung and so forth. The resulting physical heaviness is precisely what you might expect from smoking sugar and sheep shit – i.e. carbon-monoxide poisoning. (There is an alternative theory, that *churrus* comes from low-grade plants, yielding a high proportion of cannabidiol, a compound which modifies the effect of tetrahydrocannabinol — the active ingredient — and, in particular, reduces its euphoric quality.)

Leaving aside the unpleasant side-effects of adulterated Asiatic dope, the different characteristic effects of dope cluster around two patterns of use. The first pattern of use, the one Eddy favoured, is smoking or eating dope not more often than every third or fourth day. Whereas alcohol breaks down rapidly inside the human body, leaving only after-effects — hangover — dope is not broken down, involves no hangover, and takes several weeks to be completely voided from the bloodstream. The effect of a single dose is still detectable up to forty-eight hours later. But by using dope only at three day intervals you give yourself long enough for the previous dose to have largely worn off, so that each time you smoke it, it acts as a mind stimulant. Consciousness is not so much expanded, but slightly shifted. All one's sensations are sharpened – cannabis stimulates the sensory nerves – and perceptions seem as exciting and new as if never before experienced. Ideas take on a grandeur and complexity and immediacy they did not possess previously. If you note down these ideas you will discover next day that they were triumphantly commonplace but during the first onrush of intoxication they seem unprecedentedly exciting, coming in on you like sensurround. One idea flows deliriously into the next. Concentration becomes difficult and you lose all track of time. The simplest tasks become complicated. Perhaps because you seem to be experiencing things with all the freshness of a child's vision, you may find yourself thinking about your own childhood, and recollecting childhood incidents you thought you had forgotten.

Dope is somewhat anti-social. Typically, when people get stoned in small groups, ritualistically passing around the joint, they soon fall silent, as much oppressed by their own superlative mental processes as afraid of uncouthly interrupting the thoughts of their companions. With a certain amount of practice however, it is possible to have long, animated conversations while stoned, but too often one person becomes fascinated by some part of what another person has said, his mind hares off at a tangent and the conversation collapses into a series of unrelated monologues. In fact it is probably best to get stoned on your own. If you have before you some absorbing object of attention, the tendency of the mind to wander is overcome; for example dope makes it easier to concentrate on watching a film, and can make even a quite banal film seem complex, profound and poignantly vivid.

Dope makes you feel extraordinarily suggestible so that you begin to feel you might commit some outstandingly rash act, prompted by some stoned whim. Dope also has a number of short-term physiological effects, such as a craving for food — known as *the munchies* — an increased heart rate, an increased tendency to sweat, a desire to piss, and because of your increased susceptibility to auto-suggestion you will often feel that your heart is racing out of control, that you are sweating like a pig, and are on the point of wetting yourself. With experience it is possible to banish these physical suggestions from your mind altogether. Though dope commonly makes you feel passive, its properties of enhancing suggestibility means that it can also have quite the reverse effect. If you are determined to behave in a manic fashion, dope will enable you to behave even more manically than normal. In Malaya and the Philippines it was at one time customary for Moslem fanatics to get stoned before going into battle, and today West Indians use dope to give them the energy needed for particularly arduous physical labour, or for dancing.

Because of your mental exhilaration, and heightened nervous awareness sensibility and perhaps also because of an underlying physical uneasiness, you tend to feel very *conspicuous* when stoned. Standing on a street corner, thinking paranoidly that everyone can tell you are stoned, is a common instance of this. In fact it is often quite impossible to tell if someone is stoned or not. A room full of young hippies locked in dreamy silence, or giggling in inane unison, might indicate hashish, but on your own however stoned you might feel, it will not be evident to strangers. The only outward physical change is that the blood vessels in your eyes enlarge, giving your eyes a bloodshot appearance, which might equally well be caused by alcohol or sleeplessness. Though your voice might seem odd-sounding to your own ears, and you might worry that you are speaking nonsense, the person you are speaking to is unlikely to notice any more than that you seem a little preoccupied. Nevertheless some people do develop certain individual behaviour patterns when stoned. They become aggressive or begin talking insistently about favourite obsessions, be it money or women, but only those who know them well will come to recognize these symptoms. If you are alone, you may notice that your ability to judge the passage of time without checking your watch is enhanced, but your sense of direction has become confused. If you are in a situation where you need to switch from speaking one language to speaking another you may find that this has become difficult. A few individuals, even if accustomed to more dangerous drugs such as heroin or amphetamines, find the subjective effects of hashish so disagreeable that they have had to give up using it.

If smoked, dope begins to have an effect after about three minutes. If eaten it takes two or three hours. The effects described last up to four hours, at the end of which you begin to feel extremely tired. If you then go to bed, you will usually sleep soundly, perhaps waking up briefly six hours after smoking, as if six hours marked some sort of physiological transition. In the morning there will be nothing like the hangover experienced from alcohol. You will however feel mentally and physically lethargic. Ideally you should spend the day reading, or on a long train journey. Your mind will no longer seem excited almost out of control, but it will still seem inclined to drift, still seem, in a slower, more mellow, more relaxed way, to contemplate complexities and subtleties.

The following day you will feel quite the reverse. The cannabis in your bloodstream will by now have been reduced to manageable proportions, and is now sufficient merely to give edge and relish to your perceptions. In contrast to the lethargy of the previous twenty-four hours, you will feel fit and energetic, mentally and physically, confident, almost clairvoyant, capable of any intellectual task.

If you smoke dope again at this stage you will go through more or less the same sequence, but if you do not wait this long — and most users would not wait — but instead smoke dope again only a day after smoking it the last time, you involve yourself in a quite different pattern. The mental turbulence of the first hours is much reduced, and after a few days of regular smoking you almost completely cease to experience the delusory sense of the importance and novelty of your own ideas. In fact you will cease even to have many ideas. You will be overcome by a strong sense of physical and mental lassitude amounting almost to prostration. People who like to bound out of bed in the morning and like to have that extra 5 m.p.h. as they rush through their day, tend to find this lassitude disagreeable, but lots of people find it suits them. At least they feel relaxed, and providing they have not smoked too much, they can involve themselves with tasks involving a sort of surface mental concentration, such as woodwork or motorcar maintenance. They can carry on contentedly, smoking a joint every five or six hours, day in, day out. Characteristically people who use dope in this fashion tend to be quite heavy users of legal cigarettes, and also like booze. People like Eddy who preferred a heavy hit not oftener than two or three times a week frequently don't use tobacco at all, dislike joints, claim that the nicotine counteracts the effect of the cannabis, and smoke their dope neat in pipes or bongs. Doubtless these two patterns of use are exactly analogous to the traditional division of the human race into those who wake up in the morning two drinks ahead, and those who wake up two drinks behind.

Chapter VI
MOVING TIME

After another couple of years with Albert, Eddy's life began to fall apart. It was as if his relationship with Albert was like a marriage, in which husband and wife continue to grow and develop separately, till they realize they have become two completely different people from their earlier selves, the two rash youngsters who pledged themselves for life.

As he became more experienced, Eddy developed a taste for

subtlety and razor-edge timing in his business transactions. He invented schemes of increasing complexity. He sat in corners with an electronic calculator and costed projects. He began selling church items *in situ*, even pews, to minimize investment in transport and storage, and he made it a policy to get customers to provide their own transport and labour for collections. He found a market for a guaranteed steady supply of chapel chairs at only three-fifths the regular customer price and ran around trying to maintain a steady supply, because selling all the chairs he could get at only a hundred per cent profit was better business than not having so many chairs but having to store them in the hope of being able to sell some in dribs and drabs at two hundred per cent profit. He talked of keeping the accounts of the workshop separate from the buying and selling side of the business. He spent Sunday afternoons when he had nothing better to do drawing up graphs showing income and outgoings in black and red ink.

And more and more he began to feel that Albert's style of doing business was incompatible with his own. He began to see that for Albert, business was mainly an opportunity to use his charm to manipulate people. It was not that he manipulated people for any specific worthwhile purpose, it was just that he seemed to be kept going by a sense of his own power over others. He loved having people come to him to ask him to do things. Though privately he sneered about his customers, he fed on the flattery of their deference to his expertise. He even enjoyed it when they came round to demand why the table they had brought in to be repaired hadn't been finished yet, why the stained glass they had paid for five months earlier hadn't been delivered. Obviously praise was more welcome than complaints but the chief thing was to be sought out, to be paid attention to, and the angrier the customer, the greater the scope for Albert's charm. And he loved having his men pay court to him too. He revelled in having them queue up and ask for their wages, and even when he didn't have enough cash on him to pay more than half a week's wages, what he gave he gave with the air of a prince conferring princely bounty. He spent long hours exuding charm on the end of the telephone, the office crowded with men waiting for instructions, basking in the sensation of having, not only the person trapped on the other end of the line hanging on his words, but also the office full of men waiting impatiently for him to ring off and grant them the gift of his attention. He loved the telephone. It not only gave him an excuse to break off in the middle of what he was saying to people in the office, he could also tell the person on the other end of the line to "hold on" and keep them waiting while he did something else; and furthermore the secretary, whose job it was to answer the phone anyway, would be unable to get on with her other tasks because of the telephone flex draped across the desk in front of her face.

Needless to say, Albert was bored by all Eddy's ideas. Time and again he objected to Eddy selling things too cheaply. He would rather not pay his men's wages than let something go at what he thought "the wrong price", irrespective of how little he had paid for the item in the first place. He positively sickened Eddy with all his talk of prices. He seemed to think prices were more important than profits. He even decided to open an antique shop, so as to be able to get "the right price" for his better quality gear. Eddy objected, "There's already too many antique shops in London." But Albert said, "We can afford the investment at the moment. And if it don't work out, OK, we can sell it." But he grossly underestimated both the cost of fitting out the shop and the time that it would take, and for three months all the money coming into the firm, and all the firm's workshop labour, were diverted into getting the shop ready. And the more it cost, and the longer it took, the more Eddy was convinced the shop wouldn't even pay its weekly running expenses. He began to see that though Albert prattled glibly about money, what he was really after was status. For too long he had been running his business from a scruffy mews in the seediest part of Camden Town. What he wanted was to join the club of those who had real antique shops, with big plate-glass windows and his name up above in gilt Edwardian-style lettering.

During these months of preparing the shop, Albert's fascination for Eddy began to dissolve. Partly it was because Albert immersed himself in the work on the shop so that an even larger part of the buying and selling had to be done by Eddy, who saw all the proceeds being wasted on a project he knew was doomed to failure. But he also thought Albert was becoming even more cavalier in dismissing his best suggestions and interfering with his most ingenious arrangements.

Normally Albert was the best tempered of men. Eddy began to bolster his own disintegrating morale by making Albert lose his temper, by unexpected retorts and sudden obstinacies. But though Eddy picked the quarrels, it was he himself, not Albert, who brooded about them afterwards. He began to wonder if he should leave the job. Though not capable of Albert's insane spurts of hard work and genius for extricating himself from tight spots, Eddy knew that he could handle a crisis and — unlike Albert — also that he could see them coming in time to avoid them. Yet somehow he could not summon up the courage to do the obvious thing and set up in business on his own. Partly perhaps it was that he couldn't have lived with his own sense of having let down Albert by walking out on him. But basically he simply lacked the nerve. Perhaps dope, which disposes a man to deal gently with life, had already bluntened the edge of his will — though certainly he was determined enough in the conduct of his daily affairs — or perhaps dope had already convinced him that there was more to life than running around after used ten pound notes. Perhaps he even found a kind of psychological security in being a subordinate, free to leave at any time, without any real commitment to employees and clients.

He was also going through a bad phase in his private life, for he was half in love with Chrissie, Albert's lady. Albert was fond of saying things like, "Women are all the same, they just have different faces so the men can tell them apart," but his energy and confidence made him attractive to women, though his instinct for making people hang around waiting for him to confer the gift of his attention was bound to be especially humiliating for a girlfriend. He and Chrissie had been quarrelling, on the point of splitting up, for months. Because of this, Eddy thought there must be a chance for himself and, more and more obsessed by the idea that he was a better man in every way — better businessman, better boyfriend, better human being — he was driven even deeper into frustration by Chrissie's not making a final break with Albert and transferring herself to him.

It was not that he was simply in need of a hole to come in. There was no shortage of women in London, even though the best-looking ones always seemed to be further down the platform on the underground when the tube stopped. But in the mornings when he lay under a rumpled coverlet in his latest girl's bed, half-disgusted with himself, and with her, but trying to enjoy the contrast provided by his dirty work clothes strewn across the neat Habitat furniture (which he disparaged as inferior value to antique gear, but quite liked all the same) it was still Chrissie he would be thinking of. And, on the way across Tower Bridge to the church in Jamaica Road he was clearing during this period, he would often pause to throw the previous night's rubbers into the river so that they would be carried down to the sea where his sperm would mingle with the sperm of countless husbands and fiancés and commercial travellers who, in the privacy of toilets less likely to get blocked up than his girlfriend's, had also committed their spirit to the deep, and he would feel suddenly bitter at the thought that, at that precise moment, Albert and Chrissie were probably thumping around in a last-minute breakfast-time fuck. He even, merely in the hope of seeing Chrissie with no clothes on, used to go round to her basement flat in Kentish Town to roust Albert out of bed on the mornings he was late for appointments, and would sit on the end of the bed, the reek of crutch and coupling heavy in the airless basement room, talking with secret desperation to Albert about business while trying not to be too obvious in watching Chrissie, a hand-towel held demurely to her front, sorting out her clothes before going to the bathroom to dress. "I really ought to get a dressing-gown," Chrissie remarked one morning, "Though I daresay Eddy would be able to see through that too, unless it was made of asbestos." Not that she seemed to mind. Albert didn't seem to mind either, but that only made it worse.

But what obsessed Eddy most was the idea that he needed to break out, take control of his life. "I've only got a few years left of being young and I mustn't waste it," he told himself. He was convinced there was going to be a revolution in England by the time he was sixty, and he'd be too old to take any positive part in it, so that in fact it would ruin anything he had built up for his old age. But even apart from that he thought the only time that counted was *right now*. More and more he felt he had to do something with his life, and do it *immediately*. He began to think of himself as a man who had been warned by doctors that he had only one year to live, so that he had to commit himself to going out single-mindedly after what he wanted. The only trouble was he didn't know what he wanted. Happiness? A new reality? He began to think in terms of *finding himself*. He even developed a theory that if one only did the things that came one's way, one is a person created by circumstances, whereas if one turns aside, one finds one's true self. In life, he thought, one is faced with lots of turnings off the main road, some very big, with lots of signposts, which most people take, others very small, which people tend to ignore, because they seem too difficult, too narrow. But it is along these narrow tracks that one comes nearest to the truth about oneself, that one can find the trail of one's destiny and follow it most closely. He wanted to find such a narrow track and wander along it. But things were so confused, he was going too fast along the main highway, he could not see any side turnings.

And then it happened, he saw a side turning coming early enough to plan his turn-off.

It is important to appreciate how miserable and frustrated Eddy was feeling, in order to understand what he did next. The former hatchet-man for a Notting Hill rack-renter, he had no pansy guilt feelings about hurting people he didn't know, and as an antique-dealer he had no uneasiness about misleading customers and sellers about the real or potential value of the antiques he dealt in. And he had no compunction about cheating the Inland Revenue. But it had never been his way to say what he didn't mean to his friends, or to scheme behind their backs. Like Albert and all the other people he knew well, he wanted to be trusted by the people he lived amongst. But as it happened, when Eddy's big opportunity to cheat Albert presented itself, it came along all mixed up with an additional reason, which taken together with all the rest of his bitterness and irritation, was decisive.

By 1973, Albert's company had the church stripping business in the Diocese of London virtually sewn up, but on every side — in the Dioceses of Southwark, Chelmsford, Oxford — they were coming up against the competition of a firm which, from an original base in Liverpool, had established an almost nationwide business in church fittings. This firm regularly sent containers of their best gear to Los Angeles, and had valuable contacts in Rotterdam, Cologne, Zurich and even Melbourne. The owner, Caleb Smith, knew a great deal about art – especially Victorian art – and didn't hesitate to lay out large sums of money where necessary. Albert's business had expanded rapidly on the basis of minimal outlay and big returns, and Albert had neither the expertise nor even the experience to invest large sums of money on his stock. Whatever the potential value of a picture or a piece of furniture, he either bought it dirt cheap or not at all. And he was now so far in hock paying for his new shop, he was having difficulty in finding the money even to replace the stock he sold.

Caleb Smith was notoriously as bent as a nine bob note. He was the kind of man who used the world as his toilet. But he was not dangerous as far as Albert was concerned, for he had neither the money to invest in systematically undermining Albert's business, nor the time to spare for building up a solid network of contacts in London and the Home Counties. If anything, it seemed he was hanging on to Southwark only by his fingertips, and with a bit of effort — and a willingness to pay a decent price for church furniture, for once in his life — Albert could probably have displaced him south of the Thames. But Albert talked with his usual airiness of the destructiveness of competition. He needed love, attention, the sense of everyone being on his side. And so of course he wanted Caleb Smith on his side too. Caleb Smith's reputation for doing the dirty on his business associates merely increased the attraction he had for Albert. It was as if Albert needed to prove himself not merely by winning over Caleb Smith, but by also showing the world that Caleb Smith liked him so much, he didn't even try to swindle him. He met Smith several times to discuss some kind of informal partnership. "A *cartel*, he calls it," he reported to Eddy, relishing the unfamiliar word, as if it demonstrated his entry into a superior grade of business dealing. "Of course I know he's a crook. But he's got a lot on his plate. There's lots of business he can push my way, and I daresay I can pull a fast one on him if it comes to that." Eddy began to feel more and more excluded, for he guessed the new arrangement would mean virtual demotion to errand boy for himself, because Caleb Smith was bound to want a full share of the London Diocese business. When Albert announced that Smith was coming over to their warehouse to look over their gear for anything suitable for his next Los Angeles container, Eddy decided to act.

He had picked up quite a fair knowledge of art history, and he had identified a picture purchased from a church in Rochester as a Goya. It was rather similar in style to other of Goya's later religious pieces such as *The Agony in the Garden* and *The Last Communion of St. Joseph of Calasanz*, but Eddy had originally told Albert what he had thought at the time, that it was merely a Victorian daub in poor condition, possibly not even a hundred years old, and Albert had taken his word for it. Eddy checked the will of the man who had donated the picture to the church in the 1880s, and also the will of the man's father, and they left no doubt as to the picture's authenticity. If Caleb Smith saw it, even though he might not recognize the painter, he would recognize its quality and distinction. Perhaps he would try to get it off Albert for peanuts, or they would sell it together for a nice profit, none of which would come Eddy's way.

He thought about it from every angle, working alone one evening in a church in Bethnal Green they were clearing. There was rather a nice font, with a marble angel at the front if it, and he had come in to try and move this angel. He had to chip away at the cement holding the angel to the floor. Every now and then he would experimentally insert a wrecking bar, to see if he could shift the thing. One of the other men had broken up all but one aisle of pews, and in the opened-up space of the floor there was, here a pile of planks, there a heap of rubbish, and some of the longer planks were propped up against the gallery, so that at first glance the interior of the church looked like a warehouse, or even a factory. And then you noticed the stained-glass windows, and the evening sunlight streaming through them casting coloured patterns on the rubbish-strewn floor. They had broken out the choir screens, which were now propped against the east ends of the aisles, giving an unfamiliar sense of space in the sanctuary. The sanctuary rails had been ripped out, leaving a row of ragged holes in the concrete floor, and the high altar had been moved down from its place. The day before Eddy had brought a girl here and fucked her on a blanket spread on the sanctuary floor. She had been most impressed by this, but Eddy knew he was getting bored with the whole business. He decided to skip. The Goya picture would give him enough to live on for years. He thought it was about time he got away from the dirt and the mildew and the tatty Victorian church furnishings, about time he saw a bit of the world.

It was dark by the time he left the church. After he had padlocked the main doors he paused on the steps, taking a last look around. From where he stood he could see a shadowy wasteland of railway yards and a glimpse of canal in the yellow lamplight. On the other side of the canal there were streets and houses and beyond them, rising like the ragged edges of a bombed-out amphitheatre, great buildings with row upon row of illuminated windows like lights flashing on control boards, some of them so tall and bright they were a kind of gigantic jewellery, the tallest of them with red warning beacons up above all the rows and rows of yellow window lights. Dwarfed among them was the floodlit dome of St. Paul's, narrowly hemmed in, and nearer at hand, empty lamplit streets of neat oppressive terraces, front doors and dark windows like a dogtooth motif. It felt good, very good, to be able to look out on all this and say to himself:—

"The whole fucking country can fall apart for all I care. I'm getting out."

Chapter VII
FOREIGN PARTS

On June 11th 1973 Eddy walked off the boat at Vlissingen. He was wearing his best suit and carried a bag containing a few extra clothes, one Goya painting, a folder full of photostated documentation, and seventeen twenty pound notes. In his breast pocket he had another two hundred or so pounds in a wallet, and a brand new passport originally obtained for a projected holiday in Mallorca which had fallen through. The rest of his possessions, his record-player and hi-fi, his extra clothes, his eighteenth-century mahogany three-corner chair, his davenport and various smaller souvenirs of six years of adult life, he had left in the mews flat he still shared with Albert. He had told Albert he was going to Wales for a couple of weeks. It would be the best part of a month before Albert would cotton on that he wasn't coming back.

Eddy had never been abroad before. First impressions were favourable. The coach which carried him and some of the other ferry passengers from the quayside at Vlissingen to the railway station was almost brand new. The ways in which it differed in design and lay-out from any coach he had ever seen in England were all in its favour. The driver spoke English. The railway station building resembled a golf-club house. Inside, instead of the vinyl loathsomeness of a British Rail buffet, was an elegant though deserted restaurant. Again, the cashier spoke English. All the people he saw looked English. All of them, even the railway staff, seemed neat and carried themselves well, somehow like English stockbrokers away for a weekend. When they spoke together their facial expressions and muted body movements were just what one would have expected from well-bred English people in Richmond or Barnet. The most unfamiliar thing he saw was when boarding the train for Amsterdam. There were two coloured men further down the platform, not negroes or Indians, but members of a race he had never seen before. He supposed they were South Molluccans, like the terrorists he had read about in the newspapers.

He completed his business in Amsterdam much more easily than he had expected. Ignoring the pornographic bookshops and the blacks whispering *Hashish* in the square outside the dingy royal palace, he searched out a number of art-dealers. They all spoke excellent English. They all seemed to accept his explanation that he wished to sell the picture for cash in order not to have to pay tax, and in order not to have to account for the subsequent use of the money in his company's books. Several of the dealers remarked that it was difficult to lay hands on that amount of cash. To this he answered that he had a business to run in London, a lot of work waiting for him, and could not afford to waste too many days on the project of selling a picture he didn't even like for one third of its value. There seemed to be no question of the authenticity of the picture, though the dealers called in various "friends" to examine it for them. There was no question either of his title to sell it. Albert had made him a director of his family firm over a year before and his name was on the printed base of the company letter bidding for the consignment of redundant church furnishings amongst which the picture was included. And so, within a week of leaving London, he had no picture and £60,000 in guilders.

He wondered whether to stay on for a bit in Amsterdam. It occurred to him that the picture's new owner might take it into his head to contact Albert's office, perhaps to ask some arsehole question. If that were to happen, it would be as well to be untraceable. But his real reason for wanting to move on was that he didn't really like Amsterdam.

He was moderately amused by the dope barge, where he scored some reasonable grass, and by the unexpectedly good-humoured atmosphere in the red-light district, where trendy local young couples promenaded side by side with bug-eyed Australian tourists looking over the whores. He was interested by the size and apparent luxuriousness of some of the canal-side houses, at which he was able to get a good look through the windows in the evenings when the lights were on. The Dutch seemed to have a taste for large thoroughbred dogs and potted plants — and antiques. Lots of scope for a dealer, he thought, and he had to remind himself that he wasn't selling antiques any more. But in many ways he found Amsterdam oddly provincial. A night-club he went to, a converted chapel, had exactly the atmosphere of a dance-hall converted from a church which he had frequented as a schoolboy. Most of the people there were prosperous-looking hippies halfway between Flower Power and respectability, rather dour and serious in a foreign kind of way, many of them with young children. The music was jazz, which felt dated. Walking the streets, he noticed that though the department stores seemed excellent, with really tastefully designed window displays, there seemed to be no such thing as a supermarket in the entire city. There seemed to be no shortage of pretty girls but meeting them seemed another problem. He was discouraged by being constantly nearly run down by henna'd-haired girls — off-key combinations of tomboy and dandy — riding racing bicycles at suicide speed down the cobbled quaysides of the canals, and by the invariable sight of pairs of girls drinking together outside cafes, ignoring all the men around them — and him especially.

He found the girls' taste for rouge and henna slightly off-putting, but what he really objected to was their air of smug independence. He got the impression that the Dutch as a race were excessively pleased with themselves, and this attitude seemed most evident in their young women. Even in shops, where the staff were polite and gracious — and usually spoke English — he got the impression they were thinking, "We've really done quite well for ourselves here." They were right of course. It was a nice country, with everything done at least a little bit better than it was in England, but Eddy felt undermined by their air of superiority, and the way he was made to feel that he was just one more boring tourist.

By the time he left Amsterdam, he was feeling about as much of a failure as it is possible to feel with a suitcase full of money. All he had really enjoyed in Amsterdam was the sense of strangeness. He liked being away from England, he liked the foreignness — he was sorry it didn't seem more foreign – but he didn't like the feeling of exclusion.

Occasionally, in the street, he saw young Germans begging, the last casualties perhaps, at a great distance and many removes, of Hitler's war. He knew exactly how they felt.

He spent some time wondering where to go next. Though he had never been troubled by extremes of climate, he had never had much interest in hot countries. And he guessed that the girls in Catholic southern Europe would be more "old fashioned" in their sexual attitudes than in the north, not that he had ever been especially attracted to dark women anyway. He also guessed there would be lots more tourists in Spain, Italy and Greece, and that fewer of the locals would speak English. He thought of going to France — his French had been quite good at school, though there was something about the language he disliked — but in the end he decided to head north.

He didn't really know very much about Scandinavia, other than that the women were supposed to be blonde and beautiful and that everybody was supposed to be very neurotic and introspective. He had a vague recollection of hearing lots of talk about Sweden while a child, perhaps the country had been more in the news in those days. He supposed that one way or another these countries weren't necessarily any better than England — other than in the inestimable advantage of being different — and that how one got on would depend on who one chanced to meet. But now that his appetite for travel had been aroused, he thought that if he kept moving, he was that much more likely to have an interesting encounter.

Göteborg, where he arrived on 20 June, immediately created a more favourable impression on him than Amsterdam, though in a completely unexpected way. There was a detectable stylistic resemblance in the architecture to the Netherlands, though generally the appearance of the city was dull. The dominant impression was of quietness and orderliness. Even during the busiest part of the day there was a Sunday afternoon hush in the streets. In the evenings the only people to be seen were youngsters, but there was something attractively relaxed in the way they wandered about. The quietness and the casualness seemed much less challenging and excluding than the self-conscious bustle of Amsterdam.

The locals, even moving around in couples, rarely seemed to talk to one another. When they did speak, their foreign gobbledegook had a solemn lilt. A handful of young men just released from their military service, who were shouting at each other in the station concourse, seemed embarrassed by their own noise. There was a general air of serious concentration about the manner even of the younger people. Eddy noticed how they would stop at the kerb till the pedestrian lights changed, even when there was no nearby traffic, and how, in the subway near the station, everybody obediently descended only on the side of the stairway with a sign saying *Ned* and ascended only on the side with a sign saying *Upp*, even when there was nobody else on the stairway. Something about the people suggested, not so much regimentation, but rather a state of having been lobotomized.

And yet it was possible to see evidence of regimentation, or at least, the militant suppression of deviancy. Eddy was walking down a side street when a black and white Volvo marked POLIS screeched to a halt almost beside him and two patrolmen leapt out. They ran across to a man on the opposite pavement. Eddy had been vaguely aware that the man was staggering as if drunk. The two patrolmen bundled him into their car and drove off. This incident reminded Eddy of something else he had noticed; there were no bars. In fact the only sign of alcohol was a largish shop, like a cross between an insurance office and an estate agents', with colour photos of wine growing in the windows and a few wine bottles arranged unimaginatively in twos and threes on stands. Suppose a wholesale company dealing in cooking oil were to take over an office premises with large show windows they would put on exactly the same sort of display.

There was something curious about the police, too, quite apart from Eddy's normal Englishman's uneasiness at the sight of pistol-carrying men in city streets. The Swedes looked mostly neat and tidy, but the police were remarkably scruffy, with long hair and slept-in-looking uniforms. Hanging loose from their belts they carried truncheons which had originally been painted white but from which the paint had flaked off, as if as a result of years of being used to discipline drunks. Their 9 mm automatic pistols seemed old too; Eddy could see how worn and scratched their handles were, peeping out of their holsters.

If it had not been for the number and size of the shops, the quantity of English books in the bookshop windows, the cinemas with the same posters as London cinemas — same, that is, apart from the foreign wording — and the McDonald's hamburger bar in the largest covered shopping precinct, the atmosphere would have accorded with what Eddy imagined it would be like behind the Iron Curtain, even down to the sullen women attendants in the men's lavatories, and it did occur to him that though he was in almost the western-most part of Sweden, he was to the east of parts of communist East Germany.

Perhaps part of this Iron Curtain feeling was due to things seeming rather old-fashioned. The trams seemed of an older design than in Amsterdam. The girls wore pony-tails and plaits and little girlish hairgrips. Many of the older men wore cloth caps. Jeans seemed practically the uniform of those under thirty, exactly as if they had only just been invented. And yet though everything seemed a little out of date, it all seemed bright and clean and brand new too.

Despite the atmosphere of suppression created by the general stillness, the armed police, and the absence of bars, there was a muted gaiety in the air. Eddy noticed cars in the streets with leafy branches stuck in their fenders. Near his hotel there was a building site which had branches tied to the highest point of the scaffolding. He asked the man who ran the hotel what was the reason for this.

"Tomorrow it is *Midsommarafton*. It is a national holiday. Everybody will go to places in the country, to dance and be happy."

Sure enough, by the following evening, the streets of the city were as empty as those of a small English town on Christmas morning. It was eery. For the first time Eddy felt lonely. He thought of trying to discover one of those places in the country where the Swedes went "to dance and be happy" but was put off by the vision he had of amateur brass bands, mobs of country dancers, and a tiresome atmosphere of *ersatz* folksiness.

Yet apart from this one moment of isolation he felt strangely attracted to Sweden. It was not that he liked the people. He had not met any, except for the man running the hotel. But he liked the atmosphere of calm. After the months of tension building up inside him in London, the sanatorium-like placidity of Sweden seemed exactly what he needed. And though he liked the look of things, he did not feel undermined by any aura of cultural superiority, as he had done in Amsterdam.

A couple of days after *Midsommarafton* he took the train to Stockholm. They rattled and rolled for hours through a landscape of huge rock outcrops, primeval fir forests with enormously wide trackways gouged through for overhead electric cables on elegant D-shaped pylons, lakes with little houses like cricket pavilions on their shores, farmlands dotted with gigantic wooden barns, new apartment blocks built against pine-covered hillsides, looking like holiday hotels in a travel agent's poster, and endless wealthy suburbs of beautiful houses standing amongst trees with a hint of three cars and a yacht somewhere on the grounds — he had a passing fantasy about selling antiques to the rich inhabitants of these houses, assuming they would be as avid for culture as they apparently were for other possessions — and finally, after miles of not-quite luxury villas and blocks of flats like multi-storey car parks, the female guard — evidently fresh from a stint as a wardress in a Nazi concentration camp — stomped through the carriage announcing "*Nästa Stockholm!*" and he had arrived.

He took an almost immediate dislike to Stockholm. The Dutch influence was very strongly marked in the Gamla Stan and he kept thinking he was in an inferior version of the Netherlands, an Amsterdam with the fun taken out. It was a pretty enough city, with its waterways and its orange, buff, pink and yellow buildings, but it was also totally charmless, and seemed to have far more than its fair share of hamburger bars and hot-dog stalls. There had been an air of quiet enjoyment about the young people promenading the evening streets in Göteborg, but all Eddy could sense in the capital was an atmosphere of millionfold boredom. The purge against drunks was even more visible. Having coffee in the station buffet overlooking the main concourse, he could see pairs of thuggish policemen diving into the crowd every ten minutes to drag off some unoffending inebriate. There were lots of blacks and Asiatics on the streets, and ten-year-old girls hanging around street comers smoking, though it was common enough to see children not much younger walking around the shops with their mothers with dummies in their mouths. There were contraceptive dispensing machines in many streets. It seemed decadent without being in the least fun. Many of the young women, with their fair skin and unnaturally pale hair, plucked eyebrows and pastel-shaded clothes, seemed completely plastic, and Eddy was put off by the way they tended to caress their boyfriends in public, while the boyfriends virtually ignored them. They looked like tarts with their pimps. The men seemed self-conscious, narcissistic; and everybody, men and women, had a woodenness and lack of vivacity that was almost sinister.

He was also beginning to feel oppressed by the way Sweden constantly, deliberately probed at him with its difference, the difference of foreign buildings, foreign traffic lights, foreign shop signs, each road junction provoking an adrenalin rush at the prospect of some horrific, alien vista to right or left. Even the trees seemed threatening.

He at last managed to get into conversation with a Swedish girl outside the royal palace. He had been watching the smartly counter-marching guards in their white spats, white helmets and shoulder-length hair, when he noticed a girl apparently looking at him, so he asked her the way to the Fine Art Museum. He had already been there — though of course visiting museums is an index of total failure as a foreign traveller — but it was something to start off a conversation with.

The girl's name was Mona. She was a nurse. She spoke quite good English and was pretty enough in a long-faced kind of way, though large-boned by English standards, with big ugly hands and chewed fingernails exhibiting traces of crimson nail-varnish. She was quite communicative, though both her manner and her conversation were devoid of any nuance or hint of magic.

She took him back to her room in her hostel and soon after they arrived two other girls stopped by. One of them had frizzy hair and freckles and looked rather English. The other was pale blonde, like Mona, but much slimmer and much prettier. Things were hotting up, Eddy thought. But though the two newcomers smiled at him briefly, they continued babbling away to Mona in Foreign. After half an hour Mona explained that the other girls came from the same region as her in the north, from Norrbotten, and they were talking about mutual friends.

"Don't they speak English?" he asked.

"Of course," Mona said. "Everybody must learn English in the school."

"Why don't you say something in English?" he appealed to the two newcomers. They ignored him and continued speaking Foreign. They stayed one and a half hours. Twice more Eddy demanded, "Say something in English." Finally, as they left, the beautiful one said teasingly, "Goodbye."

Mona did not seem to think it necessary to apologize for her friends and began to make some more coffee. Acting on the axiom, if you can't have the one you love, love the one you have, Eddy tried to put his arms round her but she brushed him off. "Everybody thinks it is easy with the Swedish girls, but they do not go to bed with every man," she said sternly. Eddy vaguely recollected hearing something to this effect a couple of times when he was twelve or thirteen. Since then he had found English girls easy enough not to worry if Swedish girls were easier. But now he was in Sweden there weren't any English girls. He was lonely enough for it to have got through to him that he might try something a bit more sophisticated than this routine, adolescently randy approach and he wondered if Mona felt disappointed by his making it merely sexual. Not that he really cared; Mona looked too much like a younger version of Randolph Scott with tits. He left as soon as he had drunk his coffee.

Something Mona had said about how much nicer it was in the north, where she came from, caused him to head northwards when he left Stockholm. His irritation with Stockholm had not caused him to retreat from his original favourable impression of Sweden, but he felt more and more that there was quite simply nothing for him to do there. He began to wish he had arranged for a visa to the U.S. of A. before he had left London, though he guessed that America was a place where there would be quite stringent Customs controls, so that it might be unadvisable to turn up there with a suitcase full of money. He supposed he was going to have to check out Germany next, perhaps even France. He knew he really ought to start thinking about salting away the money and settling down for a bit. Nevertheless, now he was in Sweden he thought he ought to see a bit more of it. And for some reason he felt drawn to the north too. In Stockholm he was on the same latitude as

Orkney. The idea of going further north than anybody he had ever known in England amused him. Also he liked the almost endless evenings, and Mona had said that up in Kiruna, in the north of the county of Norrbotten, they were still having nights where the sun didn't set at all. He decided to go and see for himself, perhaps go all the way up to Hammerfest, in Norway, on the shores of the Barents Sea.

And so, with his suitcase full of money and his twenty grammes of Amsterdam grass, he set out northwards, still looking for his rendezvous with destiny.

Chapter VIII
SOMETHING ABOUT THE HISTORY OF DOPE

It's about time we said a little more about the drug which Eddy took with him to the Arctic. Let's start by filling in some of the historical background.

Eddy was not a great one for reading — just *Private Eye* and *The Antiques Trade Gazette* now and again, when he was in London — but a friend who lived in Isleworth once took him through all the relevant books, so here goes.

As already explained, dope comes from the hemp plant, though hemp cultivated for rope tends not to produce worthwhile dope. The Chinese Emperor Shen-nung – veritably a figure of legend as he is said to have spoken three days after he was born, to have walked within his first week, and to have had the head of a bull – allegedly mentioned hemp as a drug in his book on pharmaceutics written about 2,737 B.C., though since he is supposed to have lived a millennium and a half before the earliest surviving Chinese writing both his authorship and his knowledge of drugs probably belong to a tradition of later date. The earliest Indian references are much later; the great Indian epic poem *Mahabharata*, parts of which date back to 400 B.C., warned that anyone wishing to attain prosperity should abstain from the leaves of hemp. The smoking and eating of preparations of hemp was probably not widespread in India much before the lifetime of Buddha. At about the same period the Greek historian Herodotus related how the Scythians in what is now the Ukraine would build small air-tight huts, place red-hot stones on the middle of the floor, and throw on hemp seeds, in order to become intoxicated by the fumes. This is evidently a misconception as it is impossible to get stoned from hemp seeds. It was probably hemp flowers that the Scythians used. But at any rate it would seem that the pharmaceutical properties of hemp were known in different parts of Asia from a quite early period.

It does not seem that there was originally any tradition of hemp use as a drug in Europe. There are a large number of plants which yield mind-affecting drugs. In the densely forested Europe of two thousand years ago the traditionally most-favoured drug plants were deadly nightshade and henbane, which both grew much more satisfactorily in cool, wet, shady conditions than pharmaceutically potent hemp. Possibly the much cruder stimulus of alcohol fitted in better with the lifestyle and temperament of the early Europeans, a restless, violent and energetic people. Nevertheless hemp gradually achieved a minor position in European folk tradition. Hemp seed boiled in milk is listed in Elizabeth Blackwell's *Curious Herbal* of 1737 as good for lasting coughs, and as a cure for jaundice, and later in the same century it was a custom in rural Herefordshire for unmarried girls to scatter hemp seed in a place where the man they loved was likely to walk, at the same time reciting, "Hemp seed I sow, and he that's my true love will come to me now," it being supposed that the loved one treading on the seed would smell it and then be impelled to confess his love. The seeds of course have almost no pharmaceutical effect, but such traditions regarding the seed are perhaps a confused survival of earlier knowledge concerning other parts of the plant.

There is some uncertainty regarding the introduction of hemp as a drug to the Moslem world. The Arabic word for dried hemp is *hashish*, a term traditionally associated with a group of Mohammedan fanatics known as *hashishin*, or assassins. These fanatics were the followers of Hasan i Sabbâh, an Ismaeli leader who established himself at Alamût round about 1090 A.D. Their reputation for murderousness is greatly exaggerated. They may have been responsible for the assassination of the Caliphs Mostarshid and Rashid in the 1130s, and for a couple of sudden deaths during the Second Crusade, that of Raymond of Tripoli, Regent of Jerusalem in 1187 and that of Conrad Marquis of Montferrat, claimant to the throne of Jerusalem in 1192, but since they were suppressed in 1256 it is difficult to credit the frequently made claim that they had anything to do with the death on a hunting trip of the Holy Roman Emperor Louis the Bavarian in 1347. Any connection between *hashish* and the *hashishins* seems improbable. The tradition that they were egged on in their crimes by promises of Paradise, backed up by the influence of a "certain potion" is recorded in Arnold of Lübeck's *Chronica Slavorum* of 1210, but one does not willingly believe all the testimony of medieval chroniclers, especially when they write about distant lands. Of all drugs, hashish, which makes things more important, more doubtful, more complex, even more fearsome, must be the least suitable for use by professional assassins dependent on unflinching judgment and rock-steady nerves. Moreover, as an exclusive sect keeping themselves pretty much to themselves in mountain fastnesses, the *hashishin* are hardly likely to have contributed to the diffusion of hemp eating, even if they did practise it themselves.

Ahmad Ibn 'Ali, better known as Al-Makrizi (1364-1449) mentions a treatise by one Hassan who relates that in 658 of the Moslem era, i.e. about twenty-four years after the suppression of the *hashishin*, one Haider, chief of a body of fakirs in the mountains of Khorasan in north-eastern Persia, was "struck by the aspect of a plant which danced in the heat as if with joy, while all the rest of the vegetable kingdom was torpid." Haider gathered and ate some of the leaves. The plant was hemp, and most sources indicate that Moslem use of hemp originated in Khorasan at this time. By the later fourteenth century its use was so prevalent in Moslem Egypt that the government tried to suppress the drug, but its use spread throughout the Moslem world.

The belief of Californian ex-hippies that hemp — what the Americans called *marijuana* — has been established as a popular drug in Mexico since the beginning of time, has no more foundation than the notion that the Red Indians further north smoked hemp in their famous "pipes of peace". There are almost no instances of traditional use of the same plant as a drug in both the Old and the New World. An exception is *datura* or thornapple — called jimson weed in the U.S.A. — which is used as an intoxicant in divination ceremonies amongst American Indian tribes from California to Peru, and which for centuries has been employed in India as a knock-out drop and for adulterating *hashish*. Unlike *datura*, hemp is not even native to the New World. When the first colonists referred to the Indians using hemp fibres, they were referring to the fibres of a quite different plant, *apocynum cannabinum*, sometimes known as Indian Hemp. Genuine hemp was only introduced by the Spanish in the sixteenth century. Today its use as a drug seems confined to those South Americans who speak Spanish or Portuguese. Those Indian tribes in rural Mexico who have survived with their traditional culture mostly intact employ for ritual purposes a plant called *peyote* which produces a hallucinogen with much more marked and fantastical effects than marijuana, and they seem unfamiliar with the marijuana used by the Spanish-speaking European or mixed Indian and European population.

The Spaniards originally introduced hemp to Chile in order to produce rope, and one of the many mysteries in the history of hemp-smoking is how the custom of smoking it came to South America. It is possible it was introduced by the earliest *Conquistadores*. There is no record of hemp use being established in the Moorish Kingdom of Granada in the later fifteenth century but since it was so common elsewhere in the Moslem Mediterreanean world it seems a probability. The Spanish in southern Spain learnt many things from their Moorish neighbours before the final extinction of the kingdom of Granada in 1492, and many Granada Moors later became Catholics. Only a single generation separates the absorption of Moorish Spain into the Kingdom of Castile and the first Spanish settlement on the mainland of Central America. Perhaps Cortes's army included ageing veterans of the Moorish Wars who had been turned on by their erstwhile enemies; sad-faced dignified dons, strung out on dreams of Eldorado and dope.

Or perhaps hemp-smoking came to America from beyond the Pacific Ocean. Later in the sixteenth century the Spanish established their dominion over the Philippines, which previous to the Spanish arrival had been coming under Moslem influence. Perhaps Filipinos who had learnt to smoke hemp from Moslem traders were pressed into service aboard Spanish galleons and introduced their new habit to the early Spanish settlers on the Pacific coastline of America, in areas where introduced hemp was already beginning to grow wild.

It was certainly Moslems, in this case Arab traders and slavers, who were responsible for the spread of hemp use throughout East Africa, an area whose economic life was dominated by Moslems till the late nineteenth century. Further south hemp use is said to have been introduced from the East Indies by the Dutch colonists or by Malay seamen in their employ; the Khoikhoi and bushmen had previously been accustomed to smoking something called *dagga* (Khoikhoi *dachab*), either a root or a plant resembling hemp but with a red flower, but by the 1820s hemp smoked "instead of tobacco" was also being called *dagga* and had supplemented its predecessors. The timing of its diffusion in West Africa is difficult to ascertain, though one thing is certain, none of the tens of thousands of slaves shipped from West Africa to the Caribbean took any hemp with them, for they were all stripped naked before being herded on to the slave ships.

In spite of its fame as a centre of dope-smoking, Jamaica was colonized by the hemp plant at a relatively late date. Browne's *A Civil and Natural History of Jamaica* of 1756 and Marsden's *An Account of the Island of Jamaica* of 1788 both include detailed surveys of Jamaican flora, but neither book mentions hemp; nor does Lunan's *Hortus Jamaicensis* of 1814. It was probably a whole generation after the abolition of the Slave Trade in 1807 that hemp was introduced to the island, and even if some of the last slaves from West Africa who arrived in Jamaica in the 1800s had used hemp before their capture, forty years later when the plant began to grow in Jamaica they would have virtually forgotten about it. It seems that Caribbean hemp-smoking derives directly from the Indian subcontinent. Between 1845 and 1871 about 25,000 Indian indentured labourers were shipped to Jamaica, along with their traditional culture and their meagre possessions, including no doubt a supply of smoking hemp. It is surely no mere accident that the Jamaican term for grass is the same as the Indian word *ganja*.

At the same time as the Spanish conquest was fostering the establishment of hemp on the mainland of South America, other Europeans were exploring Asia, and with the rapid expansion of overseas trade a number of drugs quickly became popular in Europe: tobacco from America, tea from the Far East, coffee and opium from the Near East. Considering how ready Europeans were to involve themselves with tobacco, tea, coffee and opium, their lack of interest in hemp is a little surprising, especially as the plant itself, as a source of rope, was already familiar. Rabelais's famous disquisition on the virtues of hemp does not mention eating or smoking it to get high. The first western account of its use in India as a drug was in Garcia de Orta's *Coloquios dos simples, e drogas he cousas mediçinais da India*, one of the first books, if not the very first, to be printed in India, published at Goa in 1563 with prefatory verses by Portugal's great national poet, Camões, As late as 1621 Robert Burton's reference in his *Anatomy of Melancholy* to "Bange, like in effect to Opium," suggests that he was not well-informed as to its properties, even though he probably knew the account in Jan Huyghen van Linschoten's *Itinerario: Voyage ofte schipvaert . . . . naer*

Oost ofte Portugals Indien, published in Dutch in 1595-6 and, in an English translation, in 1598. Bange — or *bhang* — is a paste made in India from the flowering tops of the hemp plant, and initially Europeans seem to have been more aware of the use of *bhang* in India than of the use of *hashish* nearer to home in the Middle East. John Jacob Berlu's *Treasury of Drugs* published in 1690 described *bhang* as "an Herb which comes from *Bantam* in the *East Indies*, of an Infatuating quality, and pernicious use." At about the same period Alexander Hamilton observed of the pirates at Beyt in Gujerat that, "Before they engage in a Fight, they drink Bang, which is made of a Seed like Hemp-seed, that has an intoxicating Quality, and whilst it affects the Head, they are furious." Cristóvão da Costa, in his *Tractado delas Drogas, y medicinas de las Indias orientales* of 1578 seems to have been the first to identify *bhang* as what the Arabs called "Axix" – note his pretty Iberian spelling – but as late as 1756 Alexander Russell, author of *The Natural History of Aleppo*, thought he was making a new discovery when he observed that what the Syrians were smoking in their nargeels "appears to be the same with what in India they call *bing*."

Amongst the pioneers of scientific curiosity in the drug were two footloose doctors from parts of Europe not involved in colonization. George Eberhard Rumpf, or Rumphius, came from Hanau, near Frankfurt — birthplace also of the Brothers Grimm of fairy-tale fame. He entered the service of the Dutch East India Company and his botanical researches in the tropical Far East earned him the soubriquet, "The Pliny of the Indies." His *Herbarium Amboinense*, containing perhaps the earliest attempt at the scientific description of hemp as a drug, was published posthumously in the 1740s, though O'Shaughnessy refers to an otherwise unknown edition of 1695 and both Hendrick Adriaan van Rheede tot Drakenstein's *Hortus Indicus Malabaricus* of 1678-1703 and Engelbert Kaempfer's *Amoenitatum Exoticarum Politico-Physico-Medicarum* of 1712 refer to Rumphius as an authority.

Kaempfer was a doctor from Westphalia. As a secretary, he accompanied the embassy which Karl XI of Sweden sent to Persia in 1683, and while in Persia, he and four European companions sampled a preparation of hemp and *datura*. His account of sampling dope, in clumsy Latin, in his *Amoenitatum Exoticarum Politico-Physico-Medicarum* seems to have been the earliest instance of a westerner publishing a description of the effects of hashish based on personal experience: Thomas Bowrey, an English merchant in India in the 1670s, wrote of how he tried it once together with eight or nine other English traders and "sat sweating for the space of 3 hours in Exceedinge Measure", but his *Geographical Account of the Countries Round the Bay of Bengal 1669 to 1679* was printed for the first time only in 1905. Rumphius too may have sampled hemp; his remark that the degree of mental excitement in hemp intoxication depends on the temperament of the user, suggests close observation; the English buccaneer William Dampier had also commented on the relationship between temperament and effect in his *A New Voyage Round the World*, published in 1697, prior to the death of Rumphius, but decades before the printing of the earliest surviving edition of Rumphius's book, so he too may have tried the drug for himself.

Though Rumphius and Kaempfer had shown the way, Europeans working in the Far East seem to have kept aloof from bhang. Up to the mid-eighteenth century at least it was usual for Europeans in India to learn native languages, wear native clothes, even take native wives. Yet though they used *hookahs* for smoking tobacco, and even adopted the disgusting habit of chewing betel, there is no evidence that any of the early European merchants in India developed a taste for bhang. Perhaps this was because commercial deals could be transacted around a hookah, and betel, being a stimulant, might even seem useful in protracted negotiations, whereas hemp causes loss of concentration and a sense of uncertainty about one's own judgement, and consequently does not mix well with business. Its use amongst the native merchants of India was probably confined to the privacy of their own homes. It seems that the Europeans never came to be on terms of genuine social intimacy with their Indian contacts, perhaps because the Indians, whether Moslem or Hindu, were appalled by the Europeans' constant alcoholic tippling. Once the business of the day was over, the Europeans and the Indians would separate, the one to swill wine and rum, the others, possibly, to eat bhang.

Towards the end of the eighteenth century, with the extension of British power in India, Europeans began to flock to India in such numbers that their social separateness from the teeming *Untermenschen* of the subcontinent became even more marked than it had been earlier. They gave up their Indian clothes and, for the most part, their Indian women. Despite the pioneering linguistic researches of Sir William Jones and of Colebrooke and Gilchrist, a smaller proportion of the Europeans made any effort to learn native languages. Betel-chewing and even the use of the hookah began to go out of fashion, except as a solitary relaxation. But it was at this stage, paradoxically, that the first evidence was recorded of extensive use of hemp as a drug by Europeans.

In the 1770s a Mogul chieftain named Hyder Ali established a military domination over much of southern India. Amongst those he came into conflict with were the British. He captured a number of

English and Scots servicemen and his son, Tipu, a fanatical Moslem, ordered them to be circumcised. To deaden the pain of the operation the prisoners were fed a preparation of hemp known as *majum*. After their circumcision the men remained prisoners for ten years, sometimes in close confinement, at other times watched and guarded but left free to wander around the remote villages where they had been billeted. They had no money, and little food; no occupation, and little hope. From time to time their guards gave them *majum*. "This opiate is made, either into liquid or solid, with sugar, from the *Boang* tree, the produce of which they smoke with tobacco," recalled James Scurry; "it causes the most astonishing sensations. In the course of a few years, we were in the habit of smoking it freely, to drown our troubles; and we well know its effects."

During the same decade "bangue" featured in a publication entitled *Portable Instructions for Purchasing the Drugs and Spices of Asia and the East Indies* (London 1779), which was copied in a number of later publications; but these were intended to assist English traders in India rather than instruct them in drug-taking, and are an illustration of how the English in India were parasitic on, rather than absorbed into, or immersed in, Indian culture.

In the early 1790s, incidentally, Tipu Sultan outlawed recreational use of hemp in his territories, especially prohibiting to those who grew it "by stealth behind their house."

In the years following, hemp gradually became the object of attention to British medical experts. In 1801 Dr. Helenus Scott, author of the early Anglo-Indian novel *The Adventures of a Rupee*, wrote an enthusiastic letter to Sir Joseph Banks, President of the Royal Society, concerning hemp use amongst the Indians. "I am assured its effects are less injurious and still more agreeable than Opium," he reported. "These effects it has in common with wine but it is said that the disposition of the mind that it produces is neither fierce nor irascible nor unreasonable. It is happiness unalloyed by any bad passion of the Soul or any unpleasant sensation of the body." It is possible that Scott sent Banks samples of hemp, for a couple of years later Banks was able to supply some to the poet Samuel Taylor Coleridge, on behalf of the latter's patron Thomas Wedgwood, who "conceives it possible that it may afford some alleviation to his most hopeless malady — which is a dreadful irritability of the intestinal Canal." Later Scott had a doctor's surgery at the corner of Russell Square, Bloomsbury, ten minutes' walk from the small back room in Covent Garden where Thomas De Quincey wrote *Confessions of an English Opium Eater*, in which the more intriguing of the experiences described are more suggestive of hashish than of opium; though certainly a laudanum-addict De Quincey's motive for writing was to cash in on the topicality opium had obtained from a recent insurance case, and he may well have known that the subjective effects of hashish would make more exciting reading than those of opium.

Doctors in the continent were aware of hemp's narcotic properties; the Swede Johan Anders Murray in his *Apparatus Medicaminum* (6 volumes Göttingen 1776-1792) quoted *De Veneris* by his countryman Johan Linder (published 1708) with reference to people who lingered too long in hemp fields experiencing vertigo and drunkenness, but it was a German doctor, Samuel Hahnemann, the founder of homoeopathy, who led the way in recognizing the plant's medical potential; his *Reine Arzneimittellehre* of 1811—1821 (with two more editions by 1833) recommended hemp in an alcoholic tincture.

Another pioneer was a young Irish doctor in India, William O'Shaughnessy, afterwards famous as the creator of the Indian telegraph network which contributed so much to the suppression of the Indian Mutiny. During the late 1830s, O'Shaughnessy experimented extensively with hemp on his native patients, and it was his report on his work, published in *The Journal of the Asiatic Society of Bengal* in 1839, that finally established the scientific importance of hemp as a drug. Amongst those who followed in O'Shaughnessy's tracks was a French doctor named Jacques Joseph Moreau de Tours, who read about his work in *La Gazette Médicale*. The French orientalists who had accompanied Napoleon's expedition to Egypt in 1798 had remarked on the use of hemp as a drug in Egypt and one of them, Silvestre de Sacy — his name is commemorated in a street adjacent to the Eiffel Tower in Paris — published a paper on the subject of the assassins, and their supposed connection with hashish. There were also strong trading links between France and the Levant, and in 1839 O'Shaughnessy had heard that hashish was used "as a frolic . . . . by a few youths in Marseilles", the main centre for the French Levant trade. Thus Moreau was not the first Frenchman to be interested in hashish, but he was perhaps the most important. Unlike O'Shaughnessy, Moreau took the drug himself, and also introduced it to Charles Baudelaire and Théophile Gautier, and it is to Moreau that much of the credit belongs of giving hashish its decadent Parisian reputation.

Moreau published his *Haschisch et Alienation Mentale* in 1845 and Gautier's article on "Le Club des Hashischins" appeared in La *Revue des Deux Mondes* early in the following year. Gautier's article is the principal source concerning this famous club and also contains a good, though exaggerated, account of the effects of hashish.

Incidentally, Eddy once found, amongst a job lot of old books, a bound volume of *Notes and Queries* for 1853, in which a reader had written in to say, "I have been for some time trying to procure some of the *Haschisch* or Indian hemp, about which Dr. Moreau has published such an amusing book."

It became something of a fashion for western travellers in exotic parts of the world to write up their hashish experiences. David Urquhart, M.P. for Stafford in the period just before the Crimean War, and pioneer in Britain of the Turkish bath, did so in his *The Pillars of Hercules* (1850). Urquhart may have been both the first person to suggest that De Quincey had been describing the effects of hashish rather than of laudanum in *Confessions of an English Opium Eater* and the first person to attempt to grow hashish in England; despite repeated efforts his success was limited to weed producing "only a kind of abortive opium exaltation." The explorer Richard Burton gave a good account of the effects of hashish in *Scinde; or the Unhappy Valley* (1851), though he was not a fan: "I have often taken the drug, rather from curiosity to discover what its attractions might be, than from aught of pleasurable I have experienced." Having tried unsuccessfully to get high in Egypt, the American writer Bayard Taylor took what he afterwards learnt was six times the normal dose in Damascus and according to his chapter "The Visions of Hasheesh" in his *The Lands of the Saracen* (1855) experienced "exalted sensuous raptures" and "unutterable suffering and despair. . . an agony, the depth and blackness of which I should vainly attempt to portray", and having slept for thirty hours, woke "with a system utterly prostrate and unstrung."

Although marijuana-smoking spread up from Mexico, by way of migrant workers, only in the early twentieth century, American interest in the drug dates from the 1850s. Following O'Shaughnessy's publication recommending hemp as a drug, an alcoholic preparation of hemp had been marketed commercially as an antispasmodic by Tilden & Co. of New York. Tilden & Co's 1852 catalogue lists 71 different plant extracts, of which only three contained hemp and only one, *Ext. Cannabis Indicae*, was advertised as a narcotic, but it was this "olive-brown extract of the consistency of pitch" which became immortalized in Fitz Hugh Ludlow's *The Hasheesh Easter* published in 1857. Inspired by the "graphic chapter from the pen of Bayard Taylor", Ludlow, a student at what later became Princeton University, experimented by taking very large doses of Tilden's extract. His book described his ensnarement by the drug, the horror and despair it caused him, and his eventual escape. (Actually he became an opium-addict, and the first recorded instance of soft drugs leading, or not leading, to junkiedom.) A similar warning note appeared in Baudelaire's *Les Paradis Artificiels* of 1860. The first part of Ludlow's book is the classic account of how hashish saps the will, is sterile, isolates the user, and generates only ideas that are less fine in reality than they appear when under the seductive influence of the drug.

By 1860 then, the use of various preparations of hemp had spread from Asia to "the dissipated and depraved" of South America — the words are O'Shaughnessy's — and to a handful of doubting intellectuals in France, England and the U.S.A. Its long climb from the exotic obscurity of Asiatic folk tradition to the celebrity of youth culture slogans and shock horror headlines was ready to begin.

Chapter IX
FEAR AND LOATHING IN THE FIFTH REICH

Sundsvall, his first overnight stop after Stockholm, was just another town where he didn't speak to anyone. With its grim streets of apartment blocks built in a stern Central-European-American style and laid out on a grid plan, and its young people driving aimlessly all evening long from intersection to intersection in their beat-up Volvos and Saabs, it was like a Swedish-language version of a small town in a 1950s Hollywood movie. After days of eating in *restaurang*s and staying in anonymous *hotell*s he was starting to forget he came from a country where *hotell* was spelt with only one *l*.

Next day he had to get up at four in the morning to catch a train that would not reach the Norwegian border at Riksgränsen till ten that night; Sweden was a big country. The train lumbered through huge vistas of fertile green dotted with enormous barns, endless never quite monotonous woods, occasional lakes with (at most) a couple of neat chalets and a landing stage at each end, and ducks taking off from the still water as the train passed. Eddy particularly liked the woods. He peered out of the train windows at them, looking for signs of life, trying to imagine what it would be like to walk for days amongst all those fir trees. There were so many of them, even though in lots of places they weren't even especially close together: an entirely passive population of identical wooden cattle, though now and again something in the way their ranks faced each other across the valleys suggested opposing armies. And in the deepest part of these evergreen woods the railway track would cut across lonely little roads, heralded by the mournful tolling of warning bells, a sound as haunting as if it were the voice of the woods themselves.

The train seemed to be full of twelve-year-old-girls who had appeared from the sleeping cars. They clustered around the massive water bottle and the stack of disposable cups at the end of Eddy's carriage, and periodically they would move from one end of the train to the other in a column. They seemed alert and high-spirited but not in the least noisy. Whenever they caught Eddy's eye they would smile good-naturedly. There seemed to be a discrepancy between the extreme youthful unawareness of their faces and the provocativeness of their bums and legs in their tight jeans. As far as Eddy could see, there wasn't anyone in charge of them, nor any apparent need for there to be. Opposite his seat were two even younger girls — aged ten, perhaps — very blonde and tanned and tomboyishly skinny, quietly playing cards, some Nordic version of Happy Families. They didn't seem to have an adult with them, either. Sweden looked as if it was a good country to be a child in: perhaps too much so for it to be any fun for grown-ups.

He walked the length of the train to see if there were any girls older than their earliest teens, but apart from one very tall and broad-shouldered female reading a book in English, there were only a couple of girls accompanied by men. As he was returning to his seat, he overtook some of the twelve-year-olds on one of their patrols. The last of the group held open the door for him. She had a brace in her teeth, and deliciously perky little breasts.

"*Tack*," he said experimentally. His first word in Swedish.

"*Var så god.*" Despite her brace, her smile was positively flirtatious.

But she was far too young to have learnt enough English to be able to talk to him without embarrassment. For the first time he wished he could speak Swedish. These children did not seem at all shy or ill at ease with grown-ups as they would have done in England. They had probably never been warned not to speak to strange men, for Swedish parents didn't have to worry about the English suburban vice of abducting little girls and strangling them in woods. Except for the language problem it seemed as if nothing would be easier than to get into conversation with these girls, and he found them so much prettier and more graceful than English puberts.

As he was reflecting on this, a sombre-faced six-year-old, whom he hadn't noticed previously, spoke to him interrogatively:

"*Känner Herrn min syster?*"

He would remember this a year later, by which time he had learnt what the question meant.

For some reason the train – already behind schedule – stopped for ten minutes at a place in the middle of nowhere called Bastuträsk. Bastuträsk was a collection of neat, characterless houses, relentlessly lower-middle-class and genteel, a few trees overflowing from the surrounding woods, a couple of small but well-stocked shops. There were some seats outside the station-house. Eddy sat on the one furthest away and rolled a joint. A hedgehog appeared boldly and scuttled past inches from his shoes. He had time to smoke the joint before the train started up again. In London he would never have smoked a joint in public, regarding such behaviour as the kind of childish exhibitionism that eventually gets one into trouble. But up here, everything seemed so remote from the feverish overpopulated Europe he knew, that he doubted if anybody even knew what cannabis was.

The joint made him somewhat paranoid. He found that he kept glancing across at the two angelic-looking ten-year-olds, who were still playing cards. He looked at them with a kind of awed hunger, afraid that at any moment he was going to lose control of himself and grab them. After a while he began to suspect that they had observed his interest in them, and he detected an increasing constraint in their manner. He began to remind himself that he must be careful. At any moment his suitcase, in the luggage rack above his head, might fall open, scattering large denomination Dutch bank-notes throughout the length and breadth of the carriage. The guard, passing on his way to check the ticket of someone who had got on at Bastuträsk, suddenly struck Eddy as resembling a character in a Nazi propaganda poster, with his well-chiselled, intellectual Teutonic features. Though he was in uniform, he was wearing open sandals on his feet, a detail that seemed not at all out of character, though distinctly foreign — foreign in a way that Eddy found somehow menacing.

They passed a settlement – not even a village, just four houses standing in well-tended gardens, each one about three hundred yards from the next. Two of the houses had tall flag-poles on their front lawns, and were flying the yellow-cross-on-blue national flag. As they passed more houses, Eddy began to count the number flying the national flag. One so rarely saw a Union Jack in England, certainly not flying outside a private house; but here the people seemed competitively patriotic. This seemed to fit in with various other things he had observed, and suddenly the whole country seemed at the same time incredibly beautiful and potentially extraordinarily hostile. It was a fairy-tale children's land, barricaded in by all the harshness of the armed state. He was an alien travelling through enemy-occupied Sweden. He felt like a British Prisoner of War, in one of those old stiff-upper-lip movies, escaping in disguise through wartime Germany, thinking all the time how attractive normal civilians were, but knowing that any of these normal civilians would instantly shop him to the Gestapo if they guessed who he really was. In fact something about the whole country was suggestive of what he imagined Germany would have been like if Hitler had won the war and Nazism had settled down to being a customary peacetime political system, bringing with it unprecedented prosperity. Or better still, it was not a Nazi Germany undefeated by World War, it was a separate parallel development, in another hemisphere or in another dimension: a kind of Fifth Reich.

This sense of latent menace was confirmed at Boden, where the train paused for another while. After two days of travel, Boden was still disappointingly like a suburb of Stockholm, but stretching his legs on the platform Eddy saw a notice, in Swedish, English, German, French, Russian and what he supposed must be Finnish — lots of double vowels and umlauts and words ending in *i* or *o* or *a* — informing him that he was in a prohibited area and that all foreigners were forbidden to leave the town except by the main roads. A police car, with two roughnecks wearing Polaroid sunglasses, was waiting outside the station, as if to enforce this edict.

As he climbed back on to the train he noticed a girl in her early twenties getting on further down the platform. Once the train started he moved down the corridor to check her out. She was sitting in a partitioned compartment, and he had to slide open the door to speak to her.

"Excuse me, do you speak English?" he asked.

"*Yes!*" she said, with extraordinary emphasis, as if she had been waiting to be asked that question ever since her very first English lesson. And Eddy fell in love.

Chapter X
HALF WAY TO THE NORTH POLE

Her name was Barbro Larsson. She was not blonde, and she did not look like Britt Ekland, or Ingrid Bergman, or even like Randolph Scott. Her most Scandinavian features were her nose – concave, changing direction from a 45° slope to horizontal at its end, and also flattening slightly, hinting at a duck's snout – and her skin. Eddy almost couldn't believe how clear and translucent her skin was. She had pale green eyes, rather wide apart, and dark hair cut agreeably in a little girl's style, with a fringe and a parting in the middle, and the ends brushed to curve inwards. She wore Lapp boots with turned-up toes, and he noticed that the bottoms of her jeans were neatly tucked into the tops of her boots at the back, but were left loose at the front. He also noticed her tassled Palestinian-style shawl. Things Palestinian were apparently in vogue in Sweden just then. Things English on the other hand were past their day of being ultra-fashionable in Sweden, but in the remote wildernesses of Norrbotten they were necessarily a little behind the times, and as she quickly informed him, she had never even met an Englishman before.

She seemed less self-conscious than London girls. She had a direct, unembarrassed manner, like a tomboyish sister. She scratched herself when she felt like it, and even yawned without putting her hand over her mouth, though she did explain apologetically, "I had to get up very early this morning, to go to Boden."

She came from Kiruna, though she was currently working as a therapist in a children's ward in Edefors, in the south of Norrbotten. Her hobby was cross-country skiing. "In winter, of course. I love the winter." She also said she was interested in politics. She soon became quite animated. Her originally slightly wooden expression gave way to delighted giggles at the jokes Eddy made; she even slapped her knees and explained, "Oh boy!" Despite her foreignness she came across as the archetypal wholesome country girl in pigtails who triumphs in some *Girl Annual* adventure. She reminded Eddy of the pangs of adolescence more than anything he had experienced in England for ten years.

She was only going as far as Lakaträsk. As the train drew into the village, Eddy protested, "This is a very short conversation. How can I see you again?" She looked at him with a serene, level gaze. She never even seemed to consider the possibility of shrugging him off.

"You can get out with me here. There will be another train later," she said.

"OK," said Eddy. He had already noticed how frequently the Swedes said OK, it was one of the things that made them seem like old-fashioned English teenagers.

Leaving the station, they took a short-cut to her house through a copse of firs. Although they were almost within the Arctic Circle, the sky was radiant blue and it was very hot. Eddy sweated from the weight of his suitcase. The weeds beside the path were gigantic. Everywhere one looked there were masses of dandelions growing, not to the calf as in England, but to the waist. At ground-level their stems were as thick as Eddy's little finger. The forget-me-nots were over a foot high, the dock leaves like tropical weeds.

Apart from their occasional voices and the call of a distant cuckoo, the only time the silence was broken was when a jet plane flew thunderously overhead. Eddy glimpsed a strange double-delta configuration, the tail-plane seemingly at the front of the machine.

"It is called *Viggen*," Barbro said. "It is our most modern aeroplane."

She also named for him a red wild flower with its leaves grouped in threes. "This is *åkerbärblomman*, the badge of the county of Norrbotten."

Barbro's home was a red-painted wooden cottage, standing in a small cluster of houses out of sight from the main village. As they approached Eddy could hear dogs whining, and hurling themselves against some obstacle.

Barbro explained that she lived with her sister and her boyfriend, who were keen on dog-sleighing. "It is very expensive," she added, as if slightly disapproving. The dogs became silent and shy when they saw Eddy. There were four of them in a wire-netted enclosure; all of different species but each of them big and heavy enough to rip an Alsatian to pieces.

They spent the rest of the afternoon in the woods. Barbro's sister Gunilla, who was a cashier at the local *Konsum*, returned from work about six, and David her boyfriend drove up in a Saab soon afterwards. He was the neighbourhood dynamiter; his job was to blow up rocks that had to be cleared from roads and from people's land. Eddy had never met a dynamiter before. David offered him some snuff — he called it *snus* — a black, moist powder with the consistency of curds. It had to be shoved up under the top lip, against the gum, to which it imparted a brief warm glow.

"I have been to England," he informed Eddy. "You English are all royalists, your Queen has much more power than our King."

Barbo switched on the television. It showed a succession of serious-faced men babbling away plaintively in Foreign. It appeared to be the news. "There is a strike in England," reported David. "Always you have strikes. It is because your social classes are so . . . ." But at this point he ran out of words.

"There is an *amerikansk* film on the television later this evening," Barbro told him. Then she added, "You cannot stay here for very long. We do not have much room. But tonight you can stay here."

The film – *Mr Smith Goes to Washington* – was on the Finnish TV network, with Finnish and Swedish subtitles. After it was over there was still no sign of nightfall, and Barbro took Eddy for a walk.

"It is very kind of you to put me up," he said.

"Put you up? I don't understand."

"To let me stay with you."

"But you are welcome."

"This is so different from life in London."

"How long will you stay in Norrland?"

"For ever, I hope."

She smiled at him sympathetically.

"*You're strange*," she said, as if she had read about people who were strange but this was the first time she had met one.

By the time they returned to the cottage, Gunilla and David had gone to sleep. Barbro led him to a small bedroom. There were photographs of ballet dancers and sledge dogs and men skiing on the wall, and the table and mantlepiece were covered with knick-knacks and souvenirs so that the room seemed to belong to a young girl in a suburban housing estate in the Home Counties.

"I am very proud of this." She showed him a framed certificate. "This was when I came third in my class in the Kiruna Games." Then she pointed to a close-up photograph of a skier. "This was my boyfriend." Eddy observed that the same man appeared in most of the other outdoor photos. "Now we are finished together. This happened four months ago. Sometimes I am still very sad."

"Why did you finish?"

"He said I was boring."

"Don't be sad," Eddy said, and stroked her cheek. "You are too beautiful to be sad."

"A Swedish boy would never say a thing like that," Barbro said, putting her arms round his waist.

"I'm glad I met you," Eddy said, after she had shown him that at least she knew about French kissing.

"Oh boy! Do you always talk so much?"

The challenging directness of the girls' glances in the streets, the commercial for sanitary towels he had seen at the cinema in Göteborg, the contraceptive machines on the Stockholm street corners, Mona's remark about foreigners thinking Swedish girls were easy, had all kept the idea of sex before Eddy's mind, and yet he had not even thought of making a pass at Barbro; her boyish, commonsensical manner had suggested that it would be out of place.

Back in the 1950s and 1960s, when Swedish permissiveness was still news in England, various stereotyped ideas about Swedish sex had become established – that it is casual ("just another way of saying hello") unromantic ("what do you expect after all that sex education in schools?") impersonal ("they only do it because they think it's about time they did") aseptic ("a form of personal hygiene") sterile, empty, uninteresting ("they've taken all the fun and wonder and mystery out of it, along with the guilt; usually they can't even be bothered to remove the chewing gum from their mouths while doing it"). In reality, in a discreetly demonstrative way, Swedish women are good at projecting affection towards those they like, so that sex situations often suggest not so much erotic uncertainty as supportive sisterliness. Barbro for instance even managed to seem relaxed and wholesome while bouncing her naked hips up into Eddy's, and interrupting her gasps to remark appreciatively, "Oh boy, I will remember you tomorrow every time I sit down."

Afterwards she told him, "You are a very good lover."

"How many have you had?" Eddy asked: standard question in that context.

"You are my second," she replied, to his surprise. She nodded to the photos of the skier on the wall. "We were together since I was sixteen."

Eddy later found that this was quite normal. In spite of having the highest abortion rate and almost the highest illegitimacy rate in Europe, Norrbotten county was far from being a paradise for the promiscuous. Like everywhere else in Sweden, the children of the Arctic communes received regular sex instruction at school from the age of seven, according to the guidelines laid down by government and employing material prepared by the *Riksförbund för sexuell upplysning*, and having by their mid-teens progressed in the curriculum from sex organs, conception, and pregnancy to sexual abnormalities, social welfare relating to maternity, and child-care, they paired off with their classmates and stayed paired: it was just that they didn't marry.

Judging by the abortion statistics they didn't pay much attention to the sex lessons, either.

Chapter XI
LAKATRÄSK

While Barbro worked at the hospital in Edefors, he spent the days wandering in the woods. One could go where one liked, even across farmland, it was *Allemansrätten*, the right of everybody to go where they wished.

Beyond the pastures scattered around the village it was virgin spruce and birch forest, with clearings jammed with an undergrowth of summer weeds growing shoulder-high, or pools of stagnant peaty water surrounded by islets of bright green marsh and eight foot reeds, or great rocks covered in lichens of every shade of grey, green and brown. Some tracts looked like battlefields, with fallen trees scattered in all directions; the few trees still standing stretched twisted, hallucinatory roots amongst the jumbled piles of rock. Elsewhere there would be lawns of sweet grass scattered with harebells, or thickets of wild raspberries. He saw no animals, though duck often whirred overhead in pairs. There were swarms of mosquitoes; sometimes if he slapped his neck his hand would come away streaked with blood. And even in the shade it was surprisingly hot, so that after walking only a few minutes he would throw himself down on a patch of grass facing across to a cluster of pink-trunked pines silhouetted against the unbelievably blue sky, or in the shadow of a jagged and titanic boulder, and doze.

In the evenings they would go for picnics. The familiar English sequence of summer evenings was here stretched out from one hour to five. The sky became paler and more luminous, the quality of the air and of distant sounds changed, and the remote hills took on a new clarity of outline in the eery unending twilight. Sometimes it would even begin to cloud over. Then, round about 1 a.m. the birds started singing and it was morning. Returning home at a midnight without darkness, Eddy would notice the skis stacked behind the front door and the huge institutional looking radiators in every room of the house, and would find himself wondering what they were for.

Whenever Barbro had a day off they would drive northwards and camp out. Sometimes they would camp in sight of distant snow-capped mountains. They would borrow David's Husqvarna 30-06 and hunt deer. Eddy became quite a proficient shot. He had not liked to mention to David that he had previously only ever fired an air-rifle and had merely asked, "Don't I need a permit to carry this?" David had replied not entirely truthfully, "Here in Norrbotten we do not worry about permits and the police," and quite soon Eddy no longer found it strange to carry the rifle slung on his shoulder through the streets of the village. Nobody paid any attention to him anyway; the locals seemed used to people coming to stay from a long way away.

He was to look back on this beginning in Lakaträsk as one of the great moments in his memories. It was only the beginning in retrospect, of course. At the time it half seemed as if each day might have been the last, and he was to remember particularly standing outside the cottage on the second or perhaps the third evening, looking down the road in the direction Barbro would appear, wondering whether he would know from her expression if she was pleased to find him waiting for her.

Having gone to bed with Barbro before he had much time to think about her, he could never quite figure her out. He liked her foreignness: no stale jokes they had both learnt at school, no parents in Chorley Wood or Welwyn Garden City, no class accent. Instead of saying the usual predictable things she said foreign things which, even when triumphantly obvious, still had a foreign quality in their obviousness, for if she had ever once said the same thing before, it would have been in her foreign language. Once, in the course of a post-coital cuddle, he asked her teasingly, "What happens when I press your nipple?" and she replied, "A bell rings inside my little house", causing him to wonder for days if this was her own attempt at whimsy (though she was not normally given to fantasy) or some sort of stock Nordic rejoinder. And yet in many respects she seemed very English, with the kind of mindless Englishness he had regarded as characteristic of the customers to whom he had sold church furnishings in London. Her interest in sport, her pride in her extremely mediocre cooking, her notions of sophistication and good taste, her Françoise Hardy and Sacha Distel records, the women's magazines she read – *Revyn* and *Femina*, which looked like translations of ten-year-old English women's magazines – all suggested a rather boring typist from the backwoods of Surrey. Then again, the fact that she voted for the Communist Party and had rather slobbish manners, chewing gum, spitting in the street, scratching herself – and one of the first things he had noticed about her was that she didn't shave her armpits – these characteristics suggested something quite different, something he wanted to look into, perhaps pump out of her. Sometimes the whole Norrbotten set-up seemed to him like an incredibly remote provincial version of England, with the metropolitan features of England stripped away layer by layer, and only partially replaced by necessary adaptations to an environment of climatic extremes and vast distances, and Barbro seemed in some ways to epitomize this aspect of the country.

To begin with he could feel her fighting against him. In spite of the proprietary way she had of putting her arm around him and the eagerness with which she turned to him in bed, he could sense her uneasiness regarding him. When she said, "I am not very clever," or apologized for not speaking English better, she seemed to be expressing her doubts about the whole basis of their connection, and once she said outright, "I do not think I want to be involved with anyone." And yet he could tell she was falling in love with him. On his second day in Lakaträsk he bought her a small teddy-bear in the little *Konsum* where Gunilla worked. He gave it to her that evening. She merely looked at him oddly and put it in a drawer. Some days later, when they went camping, it reappeared. She was sleeping with it in her sleeping bag. Another time, while making love, she said, "*Det är mycket gott*". This is very good. By way of reciprocation he said, "You're so beautiful." She responded, it seemed a little crossly, by saying, "Don't be silly." Compliments about one's physical appearance were not customary in Norrbotten. A week later however she asked, "Do you really think I am beautiful?" Eddy, who only told outright lies about antiques, replied, "Usually your face is only pretty, but sometimes it looks beautiful and you have beautiful breasts and beautiful thighs and a beautiful *slida*" —

slida being Swedish for vagina. At this she gave him the most radiantly loving look he had ever received from a girl, he had not even guessed she could look so expressive. And, having formerly complained about how much he talked, she developed a habit of saying, "Tell me something about London," as they lay in bed, and would expect him to talk to her for hours.

He began to wonder about moving on. Yet Norrbotten seemed as good a place to settle as any. He was vaguely worried that the art-dealers in Amsterdam might contact Albert about the painting and that when Albert realized he had been robbed of £60,000 he would go to the police. At the hotels he had stayed, in Amsterdam, Göteborg, Stockholm and Sundsvall, he had to fill in a registration form stating, amongst other details, his intended next overnight stop. At Sundsvall he had written down Stockholm as his expected next stop, but it would have been equally possible for him to have caught the ferry across the Gulf of Bothnia to Vaasa in Finland, or the train to Trondheim in Norway, so that even if the *Polis* did trace him to Sundsvall it would be impossible for them to know where he was likely to have gone next. But if he moved on he would have to start filling in registration forms at hotels again, and his trail might be picked up. It seemed a much better idea to lie low in Barbro's bed.

But he was still trying to make up his mind about this when, towards the end of July, the first winter frosts began.

Chapter XII
WINTER IN NORRBOTTEN

During August, Eddy married Barbro, thereby securing his legal entitlement to residence in Sweden, and they moved into a house at Abborträsk. It was a wooden house, painted Falun red, with a mansard roof and a balcony, standing beside a lake in which the surrounding woods were symmetrically reflected. Abborträsk was just off the main Gällivare to Porjus road, quite near the Muddus National Park, and about thirty miles north of the Arctic Circle. The only other dwelling in the hamlet was occupied by an elderly couple — in Norrbotten most of the people living in isolated houses in the countryside were elderly — and this house was not even visible from Eddy's, though he could occasionally hear their dog barking. Consequently it was possible to pass weeks without seeing anyone. Their mail and newspapers were thrown from a bus that passed the turn-off to their house, and on a clear night they could see the glow of lights at Linaälv twenty kilometres to the north. Otherwise there was nothing but their own private lake with an island they could row out to, and the evergreen forests which stretched in an unbroken ocean across Norrbotten, across Finland, and far beyond across the vastness of the Russian Federation.

As a child, Eddy had had a recurrent dream in which he was alone in a huge gloomy house beside a lake in Labrador, or perhaps on the shores of Hudson's Bay, waiting for the onset of winter, and spending each day desperately felling timber and stacking logs in the store sheds in preparation for the months of immobilizing blizzards. Now, by a strange chain of circumstances, he found his dream virtually coming true, except that he was at least seven degrees of latitude further to the north.

The nearest town was Gällivare, twenty minutes drive away, around on the other side of Dundret, the local, rather flattened, mountain. What with shopping for their new home and going to the pictures — the latest Hollywood soap operas seemed to get there as quickly as they got to London's West End — they initially went into Gällivare quite frequently. It was not an interesting town — few towns in Sweden are. There was a large wooden church which — partly because of the heat in the day Eddy first saw it — made Eddy think of a British garrison church somewhere in India, perhaps round about the time of the Indian Mutiny. The railway station was wood too, and a bit scruffy. All the rest of the buildings seemed less than twenty years old. Everything was clean and well-equipped, with a curious discreetness and understated stylelessness. Shops gave the impression of being closed even when they were open; inside they were better stocked than in London, even though Norrbotten was meant to be the poorest area of Sweden; but even in the fashion departments the display cases were regimented in neat rows with little space between them, as if the shop wasn't expecting customers. Many of the details that Eddy observed, such as the electric clocks, the swing-doors, the furniture, the formal suits that many men wore, seemed to be old-fashioned, positively early 1960s chic in their design, so that he found himself being constantly reminded of his adolescence in never-had-it-so-good small-town England.

The only exotic intrusion into the general suburban blandness was the occasional glimpse of Lapps, usually in couples: short, fat, dark, flat-faced women in long gypsy-like clothes and gloomy ill-looking men. These were the local counterpart of the Red Indians.

Gällivare was a working-class town. Just to the north was Malmberget — the Ore Mountain — with its great LKAB state-controlled iron mines. The groups of large blonde girls in skin-tight jeans and striped sweaters hanging around in the cafeteria in the largest supermarket, and the young drunks with their bottles of vodka in the lavatory of the same supermarket, were quieter and neater but still basically the same as the kids hanging around the coffee bars in East Ham and Brixton. The main difference was that there was almost nothing to do, no bars, nowhere to sit over a coffee in the evening, only hot-dog stalls. There was a *Biljard* saloon with modern half-sized tables; Eddy went there a couple of times and had some games with the locals, but they were mostly much younger than him and, like most of the people in Gällivare, spoke no English. They had a tough, gamey look but behaved quietly enough, as if they were waiting for something. There seemed to be a lot of waiting going on; there was a night club which used to have huge queues outside in the evenings, even though Eddy guessed there wouldn't be much action inside. For a town with nothing to do and nowhere to go, there were large numbers of smart taxis, with signs in the back prohibiting the consumption of hot-dogs.

Sometimes, as if for memory's sake, he would step into the churchyard, and would walk around pricing everything while marvelling that he was here, not *there* in London, still selling the cast-offs of God. With its crisp garrison appearance the church was singularly lacking in atmosphere. The gravestones were an ugly black marble that didn't weather, but they were reassuring, these gravestones, in a soulless kind of way, for most of the people commemorated seemed to have lived into their eighties, and the crisp clean appearance of the stones suggested the crisp cleanness of their post-mortem state, just as in England the cracked and flaking gravestones suggested rotting and corruption hidden just below.

By the time the first snows fell in October they were driving into Gällivare only once a week to do the shopping. Their most important purchase was a pair of skis for Eddy. By the first days of December, he was beginning to become accustomed to the glorious Christmas card snow scenes. Barbro arranged for the road connecting them with the main highway to be snow-ploughed regularly and they could still bump their way to civilization, the snow cascading down from the trees as they passed. With Barbro the weather was a perpetual adventure. They skied on the lake in the dark, steering by the lights of the house. They built an igloo. They tracked animals; mainly wolverines and hares, but one dark afternoon they followed the tracks of an elk all the way to Malmberget, where they found it had jumped through a plate-glass window, having apparently attacked its reflection. Though one had to grit one's teeth merely to venture across the yard — Eddy kept thinking of Captain Scott of the Antarctic every time he stepped outside the house — it was incredibly beautiful too. On some days the sky would be so white with snow-clouds or falling snow, and the mist so thick, that sky and ground seemed to blend together into an awful colourless blank, with perhaps one object not covered by snow to indicate distances. All the fences were buried, young trees were bent over by the weight of snow till their tops touched the grounds: the sheer oppressiveness of it was majestic. At other times the skies would be clear and the woods would be an enchanted wilderness, with the snow-laden trees, covered as if by a frozen spray, taking on odd humanoid shapes. Distance would be abolished in the clear moonlight, and far off nooks under trees and between branches would seem near and detailed, like jewellery.

A typical day: staying in bed till 11 a.m. with the lights on and the curtain drawn against the winter, drinking *filmjölk* and drawing on each other's bodies with biros: then, when the snow-plough had been, driving into Gällivare with headlights on through the snow-buried countryside, through an immense army of frozen and paralysed evergreens each muffled up under its two metres of snow. After a couple of hours of normality in Gällivare there would be the oppressive white colourless drive home through the premature night. Then Eddy would collapse beside the log fire with a mug of hot coffee and wonder about smoking some dope, while Barbro sprawled on the sofa, one stripey socked foot on the sofa back, the other on the floor — no female nonsense for Barbro about curling up kittenishly with her feet under her — making faces to herself as she tried to string together English phrases. Then, just as he was feeling restless, thinking, wouldn't it be nice to live in a country where you could stroll down a lane when you felt like some fresh air, she would say "Shall we ski?" and there they would be, out on a brilliant starlit night, miles of open lake to ski on, sometimes so many stars to be seen overhead they seemed to be multiplying before his upturned eyes.

Occasionally they even saw the Northern Lights, a pale smudge in the sky beyond Gällivare, Eddy had expected them to be much more spectacular, but Barbro explained that they centre round the Magnetic North Pole, near Bathurst Island, 14.5° of latitude beyond the Geographic Pole, so that only the Canadians really saw them to best advantage.

In Gällivare the street lights were on non-stop for months. The town seemed stuck in a perpetual Monday night. During their visits they would see fewer people on the streets than snow-ploughs and dumper trucks laden with snow. Though most of the snow was taken in lorries to somewhere on the edge of the town, there were still piles of it twelve feet high in the car parks, and one false step could take you from the firm ice of the pavement into a waist-deep snowdrift. There was something heroic in the constant battle to contain the snow. It was like being on a colony on the moon, where every day survived was a triumph over an environment never intended to support life; or like a colony on Mercury where months of daylight and heat alternated with months of darkness and unbelievable cold, for of course with the snow came the shortening of the hours of sunlight till one cloudless day just before Christmas Eddy realized that despite the beautiful night sky it was almost midday.

He realized something else too, that night or the next one; they were sitting cosily beside the fire, with the snow building up in the outside corners of the double-glazed windows and the wind howling like a demented Santa Claus around the eaves, and the temperature outside 18° Centigrade below zero, and they were watching a TV discussion programme in which everyone on the panel refused to disagree with anyone else, and instead sat around staring at one another earnestly — and he realized he had got clean away with stealing £60,000.

Chapter XIII
NORRBOTTEN

The feeling Eddy had that he was living on a colony on the moon, or on Mercury, was not totally unjustified. The county of Norrbotten is in fact not only the most recently settled part of Europe, but also the most recently settled part of Earth's mainland. An immense emptiness of spruce and birch forests, watered by great lakes and rivers, it was still completely devoid of human inhabitants at a time when there were crowded populations in the valleys of the Nile, Euphrates and Indus. The Lapps, who had been established for unknown centuries in the forests of central Finland and the Arctic fjords, only penetrated into the interior of Norrbotten in significant numbers around the first century A.D. The Finns followed in the ninth century. Round about 1350 Swedish pioneers coming up from the south-west began to colonize the river mouths, and a hundred years later they began to build their first wooden churches.

The winters were no worse than in central Sweden though they were even longer. It was possible to survive. In the interior the Lapps lived off their reindeer herds in the same way as Plains Indians lived off their wild bison in North America. The Swedes set off from the coast periodically in huge caravans to buy furs from them. There was no conflict for the Lapps were quiet and unaggressive, and living in family groups were unable to match the organization of the Swedes. The trade with the Lapps was controlled by royal concessionaries called *Birkarlar*, of whom there were fifty-five in 1606.

They protected and exploited the Lapps as if they were a form of livestock — just as the Lapps protected and exploited the reindeer herds — and were officially responsible for collecting the tribute paid by the Lapps to the Kings of Sweden. At the furthest extent of Swedish power in the north, under Johan III at the end of the 1560s, even the Lapps in the Arctic fjords were paying tribute.

In the 1600s, Karl IX began to weaken the power of the *Birkarlar*. The coastal area along the northern shores of the Gulf of Bothnia was divided into pastorates and tax districts directly responsible to the royal government, and the town of Torneå, at almost the northernmost point of the Gulf, was founded in 1602 as the furthest outpost of Swedish civilization.

Around Torneå and in the interior as far north as Alta on the fringe of the Barents Sea, increasing numbers of Finnish colonists began to settle, especially after 1700. Except for Torneå, the Swedes confined themselves to the coastal fringe of the Gulf of Bothnia west of Kalix, growing rye and barley and manufacturing tar from pine logs. They were not Vikings, they were peasants — *bondar* — tillers of the soil who found their moments of truth behind the plough rather than sword in hand in the great stone halls of wealthy monasteries beyond the seas. Though they were the frontiersmen of the first Western civilization to take on Russia, their destiny was less the conquest of alien races than the patient subjugation of unpeopled wildernesses and the yearly battle against the seven months of winter.

The towns were mainly important as centres of the fur trade with the Lapps, but by 1769 Torneå and Luleå were occasionally visited in the summer by Dutch and English ships seeking cargoes of timber. An iron mine had been opened at Junosuando on the Torne River in the seventeenth century, but its production was small. Baron Hermelin's project in the 1790s for opening up the much larger iron deposits near Gällivare failed because of difficulties both with transportation and with smelting — there was too much phosphorous in the ore — though for a brief period the Gällivare workings were the largest iron mine in the world.

Torneå had become well-known to the rest of Europe in the 1730s when the French mathematician Maupertuis led a French expedition there to measure the degree of longitude. Thereafter there was a steady stream of inquisitive visitors, from as far away as Italy. By the end of the eighteenth century the town had about 600 inhabitants, living in streets laid out neatly on a grid plan. Some of the houses were two stories high but the largest structures, apart from the quaint wooden church, were the windmills and the huge stacks of timber awaiting export, and all the streets, save for the central ones, were barred and sown with grass for pasturing cattle and haymaking. With the cession of Finland to Russia in 1809, Torneå became a Russian outpost. Nowadays Torneå – the Finns spelled the name Tornio – is a bustling, garish frontier town; Haparanda, the new town the Swedes founded on the other side of the Torne River, is like a ghost town by comparison.

The iron mines in the interior were opened up again on a gigantic scale from the 1890s onwards, and in 1902 the world's northernmost railway, built along an old Lapp migratory trail, was opened to link Kiruna with the ice-free Norwegian seaport of Narvik. Today the LKAB mines are a marvel of modern organisation and technology; in Kiruna the miners are driven to the mine-faces in buses along miles of underground roads. Nonetheless, the whole area still remains a remote backwoods even for the majority of Swedes. With two and a half times the area of Switzerland, Norrbotten has a population of only a quarter of a million, most of it in the coastal region in the sub-arctic south. The land has an empty vastness in its distances which is more usually associated with the remote interior of Australia or Canada. Kiruna, with a population of 30,000, covers a larger area than the largest city in the world, in fact it is larger than Lancashire and the three Ridings of Yorkshire put together, though indeed all it consists of is mountains, woods, lakes, and a few clusters of box-like apartment blocks dwarfed by great hillsides of iron ore which have been cut down into terraces for opencast mining.

The Finnish population has become largely absorbed, though most of the townships of the interior still have Finnish names — Korpilombolo, Paittasjärvi, Svappavaara, and so on, and of course, Kiruna, which means ptarmigan in Finnish. Despite twentieth-century immigration the core of the population are the descendents of the original Swedish colonists, themselves the eighth or ninth generation of those who had begun the ancestral long march northwards through the endless virgin forests of Norrland from the Swedish racial heartlands around Lake Mälaren. The Swedishness of their language and culture was constantly reaffirmed by the most energetically centralizing government in Europe. Almost the only surviving local tradition is a dialect principally characterized by its poverty of vocabulary. And yet, in a way, they remain the ultimate Swedes, with all those things that are typically Swedish developed to their purest form, without any alloy of alien common Europeanness, so that whereas much of Sweden seems a rich, prosperous but essentially boring and unsatisfying version of the rest of northern Europe, with no interior horizons or frontiers other than the banalities of physical space, Norrbotten seems indefinably something more.

Chapter XIV
GOING NATIVE

Even after the days finally returned to a reasonable length, there were weeks of blizzards, but at last the thaw began, and when he walked down to the main road to collect the mail-bag each afternoon, Eddy would be able to hear the sweet singing of hundreds of little streams amongst the trees, formed by the melting of the snow. Day by day the surface of the lake became more grey, and more slushy, though Barbro assured him the ice was still nearly two metres thick and perfectly safe to walk on. The slush would come up to their ankles when they trudged out to the island, and where they walked they would leave tracks which stretched behind them in the bright sunlight like black serrated lines on paper. One day Eddy saw the blue of the sky reflected in clear water at the far end of the lake, and the next day the ice had vanished altogether, as if by magic. He rowed out to the island with Barbro, unable to believe the lake could thaw so quickly, but though the water was still numbingly cold to the touch there was no ice anywhere.

He was admiring the clear water, and wondering about sowing some of his dope seed from the grass he had scored in Amsterdam, when Barbro announced that she was going to have a baby.

"When I was eighteen I had an abortion," she said. "This made me very sad, but I wanted to continue my studying. But now I would like to have a baby."

Eddy remembered what he had thought in his earliest days in Sweden, that it was a fairyland which existed only for children. He felt almost sad. Soon he would be surrounded by little Swedish toddlers, for whom this beautiful boring country would be an endless adventure. He himself would become an irrelevancy, just another dutiful Swedish parent in the background.

"We must start speaking Swedish together," he said, determined on no half-measures. "I don't want our children to learn English till they are at school."

"It is very important to speak English well. It will help them if they learn it as soon as possible," Barbro said, doubtful rather than argumentative.

By the time Eva was born Eddy could understand almost everything in the Swedish television programmes, and could speak the language fluently. They say that if you learn another language you gain another soul; but he never saw the connection between Swedish and the soul. The Swedes themselves seemed to have an eager though abstract interest in the "soul" and "soul health" — *själslig hälsa* — but not much indication of possessing souls, and the Swedish language, abrupt and unsubtle, full of soft, mincing almost effeminate consonants, was relentlessly down to earth and pragmatic. It was like an infinite corruption of English (though actually it would be truer to say it was the other way round) and constantly reminded Eddy that the Swedes' ancestors were cousins of his own forebears and that once, centuries ago, Swedes had thrown brick-bats at village blind men and beaten up their wives on Saturday night, just like English people. But of course their national history had been different and they had been influenced by European culture in a different way. One of the indications of this was that the language was full of borrowed French words with curiously adapted spellings — *butik, frisyr, toalett, soaré, salong, ateljé, entreprenör, möbler, parfym, fatöl, byrå, biljett, paraply, adjö* – yet in changing the spellings they had somehow done away with the aura of sophistication that came with French vocabulary. It is no accident that in Swedish the word for sophistication, *förkonstling*, has a pejorative sense.

The one-dimensional quality of the language reflected the unsubtlety both of the society and its people. Sweden offered no counter-pointed perspectives, no dialectic of contrasting characteristics, no complex levels of paradox. It was not a vast human oxymoron, like Italy with its vividly baroque culture contrasting with the boring triviality of the Italian individual, or like Britain, a secure confident society composed of fearful and incessantly complaining citizens. The Swedes were flat, obvious, entirely on the surface. They didn't even seem to have any kind of hidden communal life or heritage of shared experiences. As individuals they seemed almost machine-like, they were so well integrated into their over-organized society that it seemed it could not be long before they were rendered obselete by robots.

What Eddy found most incomprehensible about them was their law-abidingness. Their idea of freedom was the freedom to wander in the forests, thinking the same thoughts as everyone else. The tiny population scattered across the immensity of Norrbotten seemed a hundred times more orderly and more regimented than the people of London, as if the huge distances merely increased the facility of control. Living in close confrontation with untamed nature, surrounded by spaces in which whole armies could have disappeared, their remoteness was not the remoteness of hippy communes fleeing from civilization, but rather a demonstration of the binding power of subsidized bus routes and telephones. They seemed ignorant of the possibility of law-breaking even in something as obvious as distilling one's own spirits. With alcoholic drink only available in the state monopoly shops in the larger towns, or by special delivery to agents in the villages, one might have thought that illegal distilling would have been rife, especially since with the temperature well below freezing for half the year the only equipment needed was a bucket; but nobody seemed even to know that distilling by freezing was possible.

Much in Sweden seemed to prefigure the twenty-first century — the over-organization, the sense of corporatism, the tyranny of consensus, the mastery of technology, the absence of overt sexual or racial prejudice — yet the ever-present sense of subordination to the State indicated that the future they had prematurely achieved had ingredients of the dark and sinister. Was it only Eddy's paranoia that made him feel uneasy at the word they used for identity papers — *legitimation*? *Legitimation* played a much larger role in people's lives than was conceivable in a ramshackle inefficient old England, and the sign of real intimacy in a relationship was when one showed the other person one's papers, to demonstrate who one really was. Similarly the civics lessons they had at school — *samhällskunskap* — sounded to Eddy like indoctrination, and the summer camps that adolescents went to do their confirmation training — and nearly every Swede was confirmed in the State Church — suggested some sort of propaganda exercise by a fascist regime.

Yet these totalitarian intimations endeared the Swedes to him as much as anything else. Often, in love, one is consoled for the completeness of one's infatuation by some little social failing on the part of the loved one. Similarly Eddy was reassured in his fascination for Sweden by such things as their naïve orderliness. Besides, their conformism not only gave relish to his own deviance, but protected it too. Quite simply nobody in Norrbotten could begin to suspect what he was capable of. As far as the moral standards of his former life was concerned, Sweden was a nation of virgins.

He enjoyed their self-doubt too. He felt drawn out by their passivity as if by a frigid woman. He liked the way they seemed to wait for his social initiatives. He had always tried to keep ahead of other people's rhythm, but only in Sweden did he feel that he was succeeding. Their strong sense of the group seemed to have been developed to compensate for their shyness as individuals, but this shyness was akin to the awkward stage of adolescence and always gave way eventually, and though invariably reluctant to disagree or to voice personal criticism, they could become embarrassingly over-effusive in agreeing with what one said. Because Eddy was relatively adept at disarming their shyness he often felt that he was less an outsider than the Swedes themselves.

Though Eddy to some extent saw Sweden as a vast hierarchy in which, as a foreigner, he could have no part — even Barbro's parents always acted towards him as a foreigner they were meeting for the first time — in some senses he never felt a foreigner at all. It was not just that, in Gällivare, there would be English-language films at the *bio*, English books in the shops, even English graffiti in the station lavatory (written by Swedes who seemed to think that graffiti, like premeditated crime, was characteristically Anglo-Saxon). He felt in all sorts of other ways that he belonged to what was essentially the same race and civilization, and that the political frontiers were less significant than the relationship between the continental capital in England and these communities on the remote edge of the inhabitable world. It always came as a slight shock to find that these frontiersmen's attitude to his home country was not always favourable. He began to hear about another Britain he had never known about in London: Britain the oppressor of Ulster — "Why do you keep your army there?" he was often asked — Britain the two-timer in Zimbabwe: Britain the villain of the *Fiskkrig* against the Swedes' Icelandic cousins — Britain the impotent, bankrupt, strike-shattered but still senilely aggressive nuclear power.

Eddy had his own Britain — London and Home Counties, at least — which had been nothing to do with the Punch-and-Judy politicians chosen by the mass electorate into which he had never bothered to register. His Britain was a fading memory of squats in Swiss Cottage and luxury mansions in the Bishops Avenue, of crowds of tourists in Portobello Road and trendy Hampstead types on the pavement in South End Green. As it all shrank into the past, so his life in London began to seem more and more incredible. It was not just the crowds, the dirty air, the inane conversations overheard in queues, the rushing around, and all the coloureds, and the wine-bar and pub-forecourt types in Belsize Park. There even came to be times when the recollection that he had habitually spoken English seemed fantastic. He saw his past self as a completely different individual, and was unable even to understand the ways in which he had related to his London friends — the gossip, the confidences, the long staccato conversations over beer and whisky chasers in smoke-filled saloon bars. It seemed to have been a life so immeasurably confused and tense, so filled with uncertainties, that he was frightened by it in retrospect, and felt an enormous relief that he had been able to escape into the Lethean influence of exile, in which the past becomes dream-like because its symbols have all vanished and the present too is dream-like because it is linked with no memories.

Chapter XV
THE RED HOUSE BY THE LAKE

Fourteen months after Eva came Lars, and apart from the occasional visit to Barbro's parents and a thrice-yearly trip to Skellefteå to buy dope — if there was a scene closer to hand in Luleå or Kiruna Eddy never discovered it — their life was the average bourgeois epic of teething, toilet-training and cries in the night.

The elderly couple in the other house of the hamlet died or moved away — Eddy never learnt which. All over Norrbotten the countryside was being abandoned for the towns.

He never quite got used to not being alone in the midst of his private wilderness. When he couldn't hear the children's voices or the pitter-patter of their footsteps somewhere in the house he would go to the door to check they weren't drowning in the lake. When Barbro drove with them into Gällivare to do the shopping or to go to church (as she occasionally did) he would feel unable to settle to anything, and would walk beside the lake wondering what he would do if some frightful accident robbed him of his entire household. What he hated most of all was when Barbro would announce darkly, "I wish to go camping in the mountains with the babies," and he would be left on his own for an entire week.

Often — especially when he had been smoking dope — he would feel that in staying with him she was submitting to fate, as if she accepted him as part of her inevitable growing up, while all the time regretting her lost childhood. Sometimes, he thought he could sense how much she hated being married to him, or at least, having to have him around while she brought up the kids. The sight of her twiddling her wedding ring round her finger — a habit of hers, particularly when on the phone — would make him sweat with anxiety. But at other times — again especially when he had been smoking — he would feel so happy with her it was impossible she could not be just as happy also, and every now and then he caught her by surprise and elicited a word or a melting bright-eyed look that said "My Man!" which reminded him of their first weeks together. One time was when he sneaked up on her in the shower and photographed her; another time was when she announced casually that in Gällivare that morning two men in a car had shouted after her, and then followed her, honking on their horn, and he had said, "I shan't let anyone take you from me" — at first she had been puzzled by this response, but then she had laughed delightedly and said, "Ha, it is a long time before you will be a Swede."

All the same the children did seem more and more to take over their relationship. He thought of them as The Aliens and yet was often surprised how English they seemed — the way they shouted *Mamm!* after Barbro sounded exactly like English children shouting *Mum!* — and their remarks and requests often sounded as if straight out of an Swedish phrase book. "*Jag vill ha ett glas vatten första,*" says Lars when told to go to sleep: I want a drink of water first. "*Jag vill att pappa skall läser en saga,*" says Eva, putting her little hand squarely on his balls while settling herself on his lap: I want daddy to read a story. "*Jag vill inte att du skall kysser mig i natt,*" says Lars when Eddy bent over to kiss him goodnight: I don't want you to kiss me tonight.

Sometimes at midsummer, when unending day would abolish any idea of morning afternoon and evening, he would come out of the house after seeing a video-taped movie in TV and watch the Aliens play. They seemed so fragile with their beautiful perfect elfin limbs and almost transparent skins, so vulnerable beside the lake that might rise to drown them, in the shadow of the woods that might one day swallow them up. "You be the old lady and I shall be the doctor. You lie down — here — and I shall visit you. This is my bag. No, that is my pillow. No, you've done it wrong, let's do it again. I don't want to play this, pappa" — he had been noticed at last — "I want you to push me on the swing." Eddy would stand behind the swing. afraid that too big a push would hurl the child to the ground, while Lars or Eva, whichever it was cried, "*Högre, pappa, högre!*"

He passed his time cooking, playing the piano, tending the chickens, cropping dandelion roots for coffee, picking wild berries — strawberries, raspberries, blueberries, whortleberries, gooseberries, cloudberries, lingonberries — making model boats, building things from lego, mending things about the house, thinking about politics, listening to the radio — Swedish radio programmes were appalling but they could pick up first-class classical music from Leningrad — reading stories to the Aliens — *Det var en gång en vacker* . . . . the familiar stories half-remembered from his childhood made more magical for him by the still strange language and the little blonde heads leaning against his arms. But his two favourite recreations were watching video cassettes on TV while stoned, one or two evenings a week, and going for long walks in the woods.

The woods were so vast one could wander every day without crossing one's tracks. A tree, higher than the others which he had often looked at across the lake, became an object of pilgrimage, or he would walk in the direction he had heard a cuckoo, or to the place he had glimpsed a deer further down the shore of the lake. He sought out suitable places for growing dope, choosing little plateaus scattered with moss, buttercups and young Christmas trees, commanding views of level horizons of spruce. Using seed from the grass he scored in Skellefteå — the seed from the plants he grew himself was unsuitable because of the tendency of the strain to become weaker in dope content after a couple of years of being sown in too cool a climate — he would germinate the seed in jiffy pots and transplant the seedlings when they were a week old and three or four inches high. Thereafter he left them, not bothering with any of that hippy crap like reading *The Lord of the Rings* to them, but all the same, they grew like wildfire, for during the nightless summer Norrbotten was a like a greenhouse with temperatures around 30° Centigrade on sun-facing slopes, and in six weeks' time plants grew twice the size they grew in England in six months.

He would walk all day without seeing anybody. Occasionally military aircraft would fly overhead; one was never able to forget that this was a military frontier and that Sweden had more military aircraft per population than any country in the world save Israel. Once, in the spring, he saw a party of Lapps burying members of their families who had died during the winter — they had had to wait till the ground thawed before digging mass graves. Once he saw smoke rising from a camp fire and, approaching, saw two girls sitting cross-legged, knapsacks beside them, communally silent.

And once he heard a stirring in a thicket behind him, and creeping back, he came to the edge of a clearing he had walked through only a minute before, and there, in the middle of the open space, was a bear. It was crouching, head on one side, examining the ground. It moved around slowly, patiently, as if looking for something. Eddy guessed it had smelt his trail but was not sure what it was, and was casting around for more clues. It lumbered to the edge of the thicket, and then stood up, looking up at the sky, perhaps sniffing. Next it tilted its head to one side, then to the other, as if hoping to hear something. For a moment the bear was looking straight at him. Then it turned and scratched itself and shambled splay-footedly off into the thicket.

He often heard the moaning cries of the bull elks in rut and a couple of times he came to the edge of a lake and heard what sounded like the splash of oars, and found an elk grazing on the water weeds, making a splashing noise with its antlers as it dipped its head under water.

At other times there would be an intense sense of there being nobody, not a single creature other than trees and weeds for hundreds of miles, not even the distant sight of a patrolling eagle, and in that intensity of emptiness he would sit on a fallen tree and imagine what it would be like to be the last of his species to be left alive in all the world; nobody to harm him, nobody to seek his company, only the unflagging breeze. He had read somewhere that solitude is a torment that is not threatened in Hell itself: but he loved it. And he would sit soaking up the aloneness, and then he would pull out his map and compass and find that he was only a couple of kilometres from Porjus or Leipojärvi, and less than an hour later he would be walking down a street of suburban villas, and there would be new crisp-looking parked cars, a couple of blonde children in a front garden who would stare at him with pale eyes as he passed, and a *Konsum* store where a man with the sorrowing face of a Franciscan martyr would stolidly serve him an ice-cream.

Only occasionally did he take a gun with him. He wasn't disposed to violence, except against his own species. He now and then came across the partially eaten remains of quite large animals, even deer, and he enjoyed the sense of being amongst genuinely savage nature, but he didn't wish to add to its hazards. But occasionally he shot a wolverine or hunted elk with Barbro's father when the latter came on visits.

In the summer he would sometimes stay out most of the night, returning only after the dawn chorus of birds had started up. During those two hours of evening gloom following midnight, before the sun began to climb in the sky, there would always be the completest silence, a stillness like a breath held till it hurt. He would sit on a ridge looking out over the ocean of spruce stretching to every horizon, smoke some dope in his little pipe, and think what it was to be alone.

Not that he was truly alone. The house, when he returned, would seem deserted; even after several years it seemed incongruous to find a house with drawn curtains in broad daylight, surrounded by trees full of singing birds. After letting himself in he would peep into the Aliens' room, stepping over their tiny clogs scattered across the floor in a manner which annoyed him (because it was so untidy) at the same time as it plucked at his heart. And there they would be, blonde lashes pressed on to flushed cheeks, usually one on his/her back, the other on his/her side, as if they had agreed on alternate postures. Once, when Lars had been feverish, he found his bed empty, and when he entered his own and Barbro's bedroom he felt a pang of unexpected jealousy at discovering Barbro had taken Lars into their own bed and that Lars was fast asleep on the side normally occupied by himself.

After a night of isolation and dope he would tend to feel unusually affectionate towards Barbro and would sit for up to an hour beside her staring down at the curve of her cheeks and eyelids, listening to the tweet and twittering of the snow buntings beyond the drawn curtains. Sometimes her green eyes would open and stare back at him, and eventually she would say, "*Hej!*" and then "*Vad är klockan?*" Once, in the early days, she said, "You look so strange, just sitting there, I think something must be the matter," but of course nothing was ever the matter.

On his expeditions he would more and more keep to the skyline in order to be free from the horizon pressing in on him too closely. In the thickets he began to feel more than claustrophobic, he began to feel haunted. At first he thought that this was only his vexation with the impenetrable hedges of osier, the swarms of mosquitoes, the mud catching at his boots, but after a while he found that he couldn't come down to the thickest growths without feeling there was something waiting for him there. He would crouch motionless, and sometimes he would detect the tiny movements of a vole or lemming. He wondered if the deceptive clarity of perception that came from dope enabled him to sense the presence of other living creatures, however small, but sometimes he thought it wasn't little creatures whom he had encountered at random while going about their lawful purposes, but something else, more intelligent, perhaps more malign, which was watching him, even following him.

For two whole months he was unable to go more than three miles from the house without feeling that something had fallen in with him, behind and to one side, and he became afraid to leave cover, and strike out across acres of rocky outcrop, as if whatever it was that was tracking him might lurk under cover preparing some unimaginable evil with which to confront him when he returned to the trees; or worse, would follow him into the open and finally show itself just at the moment when there was nowhere for him to hide. The threat seemed destined never to approach the house. With its clutter of potted plants, blown-up photos, souvenirs, deer antlers, cuckoo clock, spread oriental fans, bull-rushes, the kids' collection of pine cones, and all the other detritus of years of living together, the house seemed in a different world from the surrounding forest. And it was impossible to believe that Barbro had ever been afraid of bogeys, and even the Alien's though occasionally uncertain, seemed never to suspect even the possibility of lurking menaces.

Then one day Eddy was in the kitchen when he sensed something outside. He peered out of the window but nothing moved amongst the spruce trees fringing the garden. He went outside. As he walked down the drive away from the lake, the sense of something waiting for him with voracious expectation was so strong that he returned to the house and, without saying anything to Barbro, took from his desk the pistol her father had once given him as a present. The Aliens were outside somewhere, with the dog, but he knew that whatever it was threatened only himself. The sun had gone behind a cloud and the water of the lake glittered oddly. He returned along the drive a little way before striking out at an angle through the trees. The feeling of being watched became weaker and finally he came out on to the main road. Two Volvo lorries with trailers stacked with logs passed, and a Mercedes saloon going in the opposite direction. He wandered if he was going through a phase of getting paranoid from dope. He hoped not: once that happened it would be time to give it up, which would make a big difference to his life. He returned home and put away the pistol. Thereafter the threat, whatever it was, kept away from the house.

About a week later, striking out in a relatively unfamiliar direction, he was walking along a ridge which came to a sudden full stop, in a scree of jumbled boulders descending opposite a copse. Rather than retrace his steps, he scrambled down amongst the boulders, though the conviction was growing on him once again that something was watching him from the cover of the trees. At the foot of the ridge he paused, staring towards the copse, which was now about fifty yards away. There was not even a breath of wind, nothing moved whatever. Just the trunks of the trees shooting up straight but at slight angles to one another, against a deep luminous blue sky.

"*Är det någon där?*" he called. Is somebody there?

There was no answer. He entered the shadow of the trees. There was the faintest stirring overhead, as the upper branches moved in an air current. There was a very good feeling about the trees, he knew that they at least meant him no harm. And then he looked back at the ridge from which he had just clambered down, and there was Albert standing there, not looking at him, not looking at anything in particular, just standing there upright against the sky, gazing out over the unending forests; but it was Albert all right. Eddy guessed that he was not even visible to Albert where he was standing in the shadow of the trees. He had to push through some briars to come out into the sunlight. For a moment he was occupied by finding a way through. When he looked up again, Albert had gone.

He scrambled up to the top of the ridge again, grazing his knuckles in his haste. As he came near the top a pair of capercaillie which must have hidden from him when he passed that way previously now whirred slowly upwards into the luminous sky and were lost to sight over the tops of the spruce. All around him on the shoulders of the ridge were scattered trees, fallen and shattered trunks, clumps of briars and shrubs mixed up together, rocks, hollows full of peaty-looking rain water, clumps of long grass. There were plenty of places a man could have hidden, but Eddy knew the chances were he would have been able to see anybody casually walking away. Nothing moved, except the restless trees.

Back at home he asked Barbro, "Have you seen anything of a stranger hanging around asking questions?"

"No," she said.

It was as if something was beckoning him back to his life in London. He had persuaded himself that he had come to Norrbotten to confront his destiny. Now he began to wonder if he had not after all been running away.

It was next day that, taking out a handful of guilders to change at the bank in Gällivare, he noticed how few bundles there were left. He had never got round to doing anything about his original plan of investing his loot somehow or other. He made a quick count. He was down to his last £4,000 or thereabouts. It was then he realized that he was going to have to do something — and probably something pretty desperate — to restore the family fortune.

Chapter XVI
THE TRADE

When, after the failure of his attempt to rob the bank at Tärendö, Eddy decided to try smuggling dope, he was not totally ignorant regarding what was involved. As a consumer he had long had an intelligent interest in the trade on which his supplies depended.

In 1979, according to British newspapers, 657 people were prosecuted in Britain for drug smuggling (cocaine and heroin as well as cannabis) and 305 were jailed for a total of 744 years. In the same year British Customs seized an estimated £20,000,000 worth of hashish and grass — at least double the quantity for the previous year — and calculated that their seizures represented ten per cent of the total imported. This would mean that the grand total of importations of hashish and grass was worth £200,000,000 — almost equivalent to total imports of foreign-built ships, or cocoa, or wheat, or roughly equal to total imports from Taiwan, or Malaysia, or Israel.

Actually the figure of £20,000,000 for the value of dope seized represents a highly optimistic estimate of the street price per ounce, and of course the cost price to the importers is very much lower still. But if the authorities exaggerate their statistics in one respect, in another they do themselves less than justice. The estimate that drug seizures are equivalent to ten per cent of the total traffic has been bandied around for so many years and in so many countries that it is now merely a conventional guess. In reality 1979's customs seizures may represent as much as twenty per cent of the total imported.

A figure of £100,000,000 for the value of dope imports would still put dope some way ahead of imports of frozen fish fillets or tractors and equivalent to total imports from Ghana or Czechoslovakia.

The relative costliness of dope in Britain indicates the difficulties faced in importing it. But the price, though high, is stable. Increases in price merely keep abreast of inflation. At any given moment the most expensive dope may cost fifty per cent more than the cheapest, but this difference in price relates to differences in quality. There was a period when different dealers charged enormously different prices for identical dope, because some of them were fronting for too many other people wanting a cut, but in recent years distribution networks have become more streamlined, and the same dope sells for the same price all over the country. This uniformity in the price of dope shows that, though it is illegal, there is essentially a free market in dope, with enough confidence to withstand short-term fluctuations in supply. Even the vast seizures by the customs have no effect on price or availability for the average purchaser.

Dope is grown all round the world, particularly in mountain areas experiencing extremes of hot and cold, but the British market is supplied from only a limited number of places. The commonest single source seems to be North Africa, from whence it comes in the form of the greenish *kif* described earlier. Lebanese *kif* — "red leb" — used to be popular but has now become rare because of all the fighting in the Lebanon, though rumour has it the Syrian army are busy smuggling out what they can. From the Nepal-India-Pakistan-Afghanistan area comes the dark, mud-coloured, highly adulterated *churrus* which some people prefer. Formerly, because of the romantic connotations of the name, it was labelled "Afghan", and there were even fantasists who claimed they could get hold of "Tibetan", but most of it probably originated further south, and it is often derogatorily labelled "black Pak". At one time much of this Asiatic dope had white specks in it and street dealers used to say optimistically, "You can tell it's good, those white specks are the opium they've put in it to make it stronger." Probably the specks were *datura*; dope of this kind has now disappeared from the market.

Grass is not usually imported from the *kif* or *churrus* producing areas. Perhaps because it was the normal form of dope in the United States, grass for a long time had a kind of snob value in Britain, though it isn't necessarily stronger or more exotic in its effects than *kif* or *churrus*. The amount coming into Britain seems to have increased during the 1970s, relative to the proportion of other forms of dope — which is interesting since, being bulkier for the same weight, it is more problem to smuggle. Some of it comes from Colombia and may possibly have been used as a make-weight in cocaine smuggling. Because every consignment is dried and packed differently, it is difficult to identify the source from the appearance, except in the case of the highly prized Thai Sticks which come as dried plants neatly tied up with twine around a small stick and individually wrapped in silver foil. It may be presumed that quite large quantities are imported from Jamaica; some also comes from South Africa. There are also large amounts grown by individuals in Britain in their back-gardens or greenhouses, though this is usually identifiable by its freshness and is not usually handled by regular dealers. In 1974 there were 451 convicitions for growing dope in Britain, and 975 in 1977.

The spread of the dope habit in the 1960s was largely connected with the increase during that decade of facilities for young people to travel to Africa and Asia. Once the first hippies returning from India and Morocco had created a market for dope in England, the trade quickly became professionalized. To begin with, apart from the odd ounce or two carried by young tourists, most of the dope entered the country in loads of ten to twenty "weights" (pounds). People would run it through customs in their cars. Eddy used to know one team of three who used to take it in turns to fly to Kabul every week and return with a couple of suitcases full. They had agreed to give it up if any one of them was ever busted, but none of them ever were. For all he knew they were still in business.

Round about 1970 there began to be a lot of heaviness. People had become indiscreet. So-and-so would have a mate who wanted some dope and also knew someone else whose friend could handle a "weight" or so, guys would turn up that you'd never even heard of, asking to buy, and soon enough, lots of unpleasant types would be hanging around your doorstep. One time a group turned up at a flat with a thousand pounds to buy a load and when they left with their suitcase full a couple of geezers with sawn-off shotguns were waiting outside, who took the suitcase and drove off in a waiting car. Another bloke Eddy knew was in his flat, having a quiet smoke when three blokes came in — seemed to be police — threw him against the wall, ransacked the flat, took his gear, and that was the last he heard of them. After weeks of sweating waiting for his summons, he cottoned on to the fact that they hadn't been police at all. After a number of such incidents, people began to tidy up their distribution networks. The group doing the weekly run from Kabul put it out amongst three or four contacts, on credit. After making an appointment by telephone, they would deliver the gear to their contacts, and these middlemen would then summon their retailers who would come round immediately and take away a "weight" each. Operating through a network of known and trusted contacts, it was possible to proceed on credit, and each dealer would see only his source and three or four customers. If a stranger contacted such a dealer, he would say, "Well, I might be able to get you an ounce, but not any more than that." Round about 1970, it was quite common to be approached in the sidestreets of Notting Hill by young blacks hissing, "Hey man, you want to score?" but with the tightening up of organization contacts can now only be made through trusted friends.

During the 1970s there was not only a period of confusion amongst dealers in the home market, the smuggling itself became far more difficult. The rise of international terrorism meant that airport security became much tighter, and with the Customs more and more on the lookout for drugs, the idea of driving a carload of *kif* from Morocco, through the stringent checks at Algeciras, no longer made any sense. Apart from the odd ounce, smuggled in by rash amateurs, and some ten pound deals brought in by sailors docking at British ports, and perhaps some medium-size consignments brought by individuals from Amsterdam — only one Customs check, and only the relative luxury of an English jail to risk if caught, but not much margin for profit — the importation is today in bulk. Consignments are flown in by private planes, or landed secretly from motor launches. In one operation, several tons of dope were landed in rubber dinghies from a freighter off the coast of Scotland. Operations on this scale necessarily involve vast outlays of capital, and the participation of far larger numbers of people than hitherto. Some of the networks rounded up by the British police involve up to fifty people, with legitimate businesses as fronts. And because of structural changes of this sort, the connection between cannabis and the trade in cocaine and heroin is increasing — single-drug business is now virtually impracticable except for the lower-echelon dealers. At the upper levels there is probably quite a lot of heaviness, because smuggling is now a multi-million pound crime, but in the middle and lower range the business is relatively decorous.

Lots of middle-range smugglers made enough money to move into the safer realms of antiques and wine-bars or whatever, and became mere users. One or two others have continued in business for years, serving jail sentences in different countries, accepting that as one of the risks, and in between living like princes. Others again have moved on to heroin and have become junkies, which is another story altogether. For the middle-range smuggler, carrying small quantities of heroin — as a courier, not as an investor — is still just about worthwhile for the money you get, so many of the surviving middle-range smugglers have moved over to handling heroin. Since the early 1970s the number of smugglers who have retired, been busted, moved on to handling heroin etc, has been much greater than the numbers of recruits to the trade, and the overall reduction in the numbers of people involved is probably a major factor in the increased scale of the operations.

Eddy's plan — to smuggle in less than ten kilos, hidden under the floor behind the back seat of his Volvo estate wagon — essentially belonged to the earlier phase of the history of dope traffic, But that was all right by him; he liked to be out of step.

And just to be really different, he decided to hide his pistol along with the dope. There was no way the Customs at Felixstowe were going to search the car of a family of innocent Swedish tourists, and the pistol might turn out to be useful in London.

Chapter XVII
RETURN TO THE BIG CITY

They came like travellers from Outer Space, space colonists returning to Terra from the other side of the galaxy, gaping at the high-rise office buildings like block diagrams showing the economy going out of control and the crowded sky overhead.

"Will the aeroplane hit the building?" Lars asked, looking up at an airliner; he had seen jet aircraft before, in Norrbotten, but never any building higher than the twelve-storey office block in Malmberget.

"What does this mean?" Eva asked, pointing to some words scrawled in black crayon on an advertising poster; they said, "Do it dog style with Hannah 78-78-88. Phone 359 4925."

Curious how metrication was spreading, thought Eddy.

He had been reminding himself, ever since they had left Abborträsk, how run-down and decrepit London was. He remembered it as a city full of buildings that were so decayed that he supposed most of them would have fallen down while he had been away. But driving into the centre of London he had been surprised by the number of neat, well-maintained (though cramped) side streets they had passed. Even Euston Road was not as depressing as he had expected. They were restoring the facade of St. Pancras and had opened up the forecourt of Euston Station, and the traffic seemed bright and new, with lots of V registration cars — the number plates had only got as far as L when he had left. There were more skyscrapers than he remembered, and helicopters flying overhead. But the streets were still full of rubbish, and the lead story in the evening papers was that old favourite, *sex fiend freed to rape again*, that they had had at least once a month ever since he had first come to London as a teenager.

"Why is that man's hair a funny colour?" Eva asked.

"I think he is a Punk Rocker," said Barbro, who had read a magazine article about them.

"Look, there is a double-decker bus," said Lars.

We're just like any other family of European tourists, Eddy thought, almost ashamed. But there had been a time when he could have driven down this street and felt, "This is mine, *my* territory. *That* church, I know more about it and the gear in it than the churchwardens. I know where to buy this and sell that. And all these other people, they're just punters, with their nine-to-five jobs, just good enough to earn the money to pay for the clobber I sell them." He had felt free — and this was what he had used his freedom for, to come back and be just another tourist, just another sacrificial victim to be sucked dry for his quota of desperately needed foreign currency.

London seemed completely geared to exploiting the tourist trade. But the superficial prosperity and the tourist glamour seemed to be only a façade. The newspapers and a hundred and one little details that Eddy noticed told quite a different story. Afterwards he was to think of Britain as being like a rotting corpse with millions of microbes battening on it and converting the dying tissues into the unnourishing substance on which they subsisted — money. That is a metaphor: the stench of decay which hung over the scene, unless it was to be localized as a matter of damp plaster, blocked drains, rotting dustbins, stinking tramps, was only a metaphorical stench, but it pervaded everywhere. Like any other animal after its death, the country had ceased to function as a single organism, and had become the host for a multitude of smaller organisms, each looking to only its own purposes. Public services — schools, transport, medical services, which had previously not merely served to integrate the nation physically and socially but had also acted as key symbols of integration — were collapsing in disarray as their funds were cut off by government. Eddy found that the papers were full of stories of their daily deterioration. But as these services were cut, the official bodies responsible for overseeing them grew. It seemed that the bureaucracies of Whitehall and the town-halls were growing like a cancer, flourishing as the metabolic defences of the rest of the organism decayed. Of course, not every area of pubic service declined. The BBC and local radio flourished, with no more than minor inconveniences, issuing a strident barrage of entertainment that as far as Eddy could see was totally at variance with the realities spreading over the land. He learnt that expenditure on the armed forces was being increased too, though for no realistic purpose, for the investment was geared much more to preparing for a Soviet attack that was increasingly unlikely to come, than to preparing the man-power and techniques necessary to counter the disintegration growing at home. It was as if the government had given up doing more than go through the motions of constructive government and consoled itself with the fantasies of preparing for a global war, which, they probably hoped, would overtake the nation before its slip from third-rateness to fifth-rateness became too generally noticed.

Despite the rhetoric of capitalist endeavour and a great deal of personal enthusiasm for the Tory government on the part of businessmen, Eddy knew it was impossible that business should flourish in such a morass of disintegration. Harassed by inflation, high taxes and unfavourable exchange rates, businesses were being forced to cut investment, cut corners, cut everything. But for those who could best adapt themselves to the situation, livings were to be made, selling the country and its culture piecemeal to foreigners. Even Westminster Abbey was for sale, to tourists; even the English language, which was much in demand as a kind of inter-continental *lingua franca* and was available from a hundred and one Schools of English that had mushroomed all over the capital.

And everywhere Eddy saw indications of schizophrenia. The neon lights in the West End seemed to have no connection with the ubiquitous National Front scrawls on walls, or with the screen-printed posters announcing demonstrations against unemployment which he saw everywhere pasted up in back streets. The glossy-looking sex shops in Tottenham Court Road seemed a world away from the tramp sleeping in the adjacent underground station, sitting on two polythene carrier bags to reduce the chill of the cement floor. The jet-liners cruising silently, almost dreamily overhead whenever he looked up, were exciting to begin with, but after a while they seemed to be draining even the heavens of their heavenliness, making the sky itself merely a part of the ruin below: and every airliner would be packed with tourists avid for their share of the London experience, yet whenever Eddy saw one, he thought also of English refugees fleeing desperately before it was too late.

While Barbro hauled the Aliens around the British Museum, he cruised around London looking out for things that had changed. There seemed to be more antique shops than ever before. He dropped into some, to look around, ask questions. The exchange rate was hitting trade a bit, and the early 1970s boom in stripped pine had spawned so many stripped pine businesses that the market had been smothered, but quality gear was still doing quite well, selling to Dutch and German businessmen, and the dealers he spoke to seemed quite pleased with themselves. But what Eddy was really interested in was a different kind of dealer; he had all those kilos of grass to move.

He traced one former contact to an antiques shop in Kensington Church Street. It was well laid-out, good quality gear. There were no customers, but the man said he couldn't really slip out for a pint, his boss would raise hell. After they compared notes for a few minutes Eddy didn't even bother to ask if the man was still smoking pot.

Someone else he traced to a demolition company in Finchley. The office directed him to a site in Crouch End where his friend was foreman. It was an old primary school they were pulling down, no fancy equipment, and the crew were mainly broken-down old navvies, all of them old enough to be the foreman's father. It was 5.30 by the time Eddy arrived, and the men were just being paid off. Half of them wouldn't turn up next day, but there was never any problem finding substitutes.

"Long time no see," said Ken — that was the foreman's name. They adjourned to a pub for a couple of whiskies. Ken looked good. He was tanned from his outdoor work, and had that confident air that comes from having a fat wad of tens and twenties in your hip pocket. He made Eddy feel good, too. A demolition foreman needs to be tough, in order to get work out of his men; he needs to be able to show any man off the site who argues, and every now and then he has to scramble up to the most precarious positions to swing a pick at the very masonry he is standing on, just to show the crew he isn't a cissy. Ken was one of the best. He hadn't had to punch a head in years, and did only enough work to sweat off his lunch-time lagers. But when Eddy turned the conversation round to dope, Ken merely pulled a face. He said:-

"Hippy muck. You can't smoke that stuff and hold down a job like mine. Makes you act too relaxed. In this job you have to look like you're going to go berserk at any moment, otherwise some paddy's liable to sneak up on you from behind and clock you one. You've got to act wound up. Coke, amphetamines, I'll even crack a phial of amyl nitrate, but hash I haven't touched for years."

There was Annette, the woman dealer in the council tower blocks in Adelaide Road. Eddy tried her. She'd always been the worst dealer he had known for paranoia. It wasn't just that she was a woman, in extra danger of being hustled: she just seemed naturally full of hate for customers. "Sorry to have to say this, but, you know, like, can I see your money first? I mean, I know it's a hassle, but, like if you don't mind." And she would let people in as if the flat was crowded with prospective in-laws whom she didn't want you to meet. But on this occasions she was unusually welcoming, recognizing Eddy immediately. She made him some tea, chatting the while. She had done a government training course in typing and had been a secretary for three years now. It had been boring at first, but it was steady money with no hassle. She still alluded to her interesting friends in pop groups he had never heard of, but what she really wanted to talk to him about was the other girls in the office. The oldest one who was always telling tales, snitching on the others. The new one whose spelling was weak. "I mean I have to read through all *her* work on top of my own. Mr Hammond told me, I know she oughtn't to take dictations, he said. . . ." Eddy could remember her saying "I'd rather die than have a nine to five job, I mean, I can't even get up that early in the morning. And every day, week in, week out, I mean, it sounds like a prison sentence." But that had been in 1972. He left without mentioning drugs.

He decided to check out Bristol Gardens, in Maida Vale, one of London's longest-running squats. He was gratified to discover that it was still going strong. During his time in Sweden it seemed to have decayed even further, but there was a positively Mediterranean quality about it now, from all the children and dogs to be seen on the pavements. Some of the graffiti was quite good too; he noticed one scrawl saying, "Save energy, fart in a jar." He began to feel better: he had been beginning to be afraid that everybody in London had become straight while had had been away.

He had known some people in No. 5. They had probably moved on, but even if they had, the people who had taken over their rooms would probably be able to tell him where to contact various people who might be able to help him. The front door of No. 5 was open. He was just about to enter when he heard his name shouted.

He turned automatically and then his heart leapt to his mouth.

It was the one person he had prayed not to run into in London.

Albert.

Chapter XVIII
A MAN FROM THE PAST

"Where the fuck have *you* been?" Albert said, shaking his hand warmly.

"Good to see you," Eddy said. And it was true. In spite of himself he found he was grinning with pleasure.

When he told Albert he had been living in Sweden, Albert exclaimed:—

"*Sweden!* Christ, what was wrong with Wales, where everyone else goes when he wants to get away from it all. I mean, *Sweden.*"

"Went to escape the H-bomb, didn't I," Eddy said, meaning to sound flip.

They drove in Eddy's Volvo back to Albert's headquarters. He had moved from the mews in Camden Town, which had long since been demolished, and now occupied a redundant church in South Hackney. It was approached through a maze of deserted streets: no houses, only offices and decaying warehouses. The church itself was surrounded by a wasteland of rubble and partially demolished tenements. Beyond the wooden gates into its enclosed yard, its bulk rose like an ocean liner against the stars. To the south, the histogram blocks and minuscule lights of the skyscrapers in the City were in a different world, separated from them by a fold in the seam of time. Reckless Eric blared out from an open window in the clergy house adjoining the church.

"Great, isn't it?" said Albert. "Every time I look at that —" he meant the church " — I think, isn't that amazing? What a man he must have been who built that — what a complete mediocrity!"

He lived on the top floor of the clergy house. His room was the inevitable Albert mess — Windsor chairs, a rather striking cylinder-top pedestal desk, rolls of carpet, an ivory chess set, a fruit machine, some African masks that were old and dirty enough to be genuine, not tourist pieces, lots of cobwebs, fluff in all the corners. Just across the corridor from Albert's door was a little flight of steps up to a doorway leading out on to a flat section of the roof, Albert's private look-out post, from which one day perhaps he would direct the conquest of London.

Albert didn't seem to have changed much in eight years: merely a few broken capillaries on his freckly cheeks, a few more pounds on his beer pod, and the beginning of a bald patch. And he was still the same old Albert as far as schemes were concerned. "I'm thinking of taking up golf," he confided. "You know, join a club, one of those exclusive clubs in north London, where they don't let in Jews. Make lots of influential friends that way. I've been meeting too many of the wrong people lately. Well, there was a big fuss in Tower Hamlets some months back about some cock-eyed development scheme the Labour-controlled Council was trying to foist on people — you know, the usual multi-million pound project to turn human beings into animals in bright new vinyl and plasterboard zoos. I got a little bit involved with some of the people lobbying against that, and then I began to worry about all those immigrants claiming Social Security for twenty children and three wives, so I began to talk things over with a couple of chaps in the National Front. I don't like organizations and the National Front is just a fucking wrist-job same as the others, but some of the geezers in it were OK. Still, the rest were just yobboes, and I've decided I'm never going to really get on unless I move myself a bit up market, hang around with a classier type of dude. Might even become a Freemason."

Before taking Albert back to the hotel to meet Barbro, Eddy thought it as well to warn him that people were left-wing in Norrbotten. "It's just the way they are up there. They mostly work for big iron-mining and timber companies, so the unions are pretty strong. It's not just her. She just believes the same wimpishness as everybody else up there. So be careful what you say. Don't be controversial — all right?"

He drove Albert to the hotel in Earls Court. As they passed Earls Court Tube Station he remarked on the number of Arabs to be seen on the street.

"It used to be all Irish and Australians here, didn't it? Kangaroo Valley."

"It's Arabs now," Albert said, "London's the capital of the Arab world; not Cairo, not Riyadh. Doesn't matter about London not being central, they can afford the air-fare, and anyhow it's quicker by Concorde. Have you noticed all the Arab banks? And apparently there's a private clinic in St. John's Wood which had a contract to patch up Libyan Army soldiers. They don't bother with having a proper hospital in Libya — less trouble to send them here, where they are all stashed away in luxury private rooms, and can't complain because none of them speak English. They were doing a roaring trade during all that fighting in Uganda which the Libyans were mixed up in."

Eddy didn't much like the sound of that. He had never expected to feel homesick for Gällivare, but at least all the faces were white there, if one didn't count the occasional Lapp, and one didn't even have to worry about being a racist.

At the hotel, Barbro had put the children to bed and was reading a glossy book she had bought that day in the British Museum.

Albert produced a half bottle of malt whisky from his coat pocket and was soon talking plausibly about booming property values, especially in Hackney: —

"It's so economically depressed there, it's gone down so far it can only come up. And the government and the Greater London Council are keen to pump in lots of money. Basically, I think antiques have had it as a way of making a decent living. They've been costing too much for too long. There's a limit to how much can be absorbed by the Pension Funds and the private collectors and the half-wits in Hampstead who want an investment. And there's too much competition. It forces up the price you buy at, and undercuts the price you sell at. Result: no margin. Thing to do is to see where the growth areas are and put your weight there. Property in Hackney is one growth area. Another is *security*. Lock companies are booming. The better off people are, the more afraid they are of being murdered in their own homes — especially in England where the easiest way to get better off is to make someone else worse off. I've been thinking of moving into the Private Security business. Quite a bit of competition there, but there's plenty of scope for innovation. You know, Vigilante Systems. People are beginning to think of laying on vigilante patrols round their houses, especially in those private estates. They need guidance, expert advice, a bit of hardware like alarm bells and floodlight systems."

Basically Eddy found all this a bit boring, and yet at the same time he still found himself being seduced by Albert's confidence and charm. Naturally he said nothing about the circumstances of his sudden departure from London in 1973 — and Albert, accustomed to his work force coming and going, didn't ask — but when at last he was driving his former boss back to his church he explained about the dope hidden in the back of the Volvo. If anybody had the right contacts for moving twenty weights of dope, it was Albert.

"Dope from Sweden?" Albert thought that very odd.

Eddy said:—

"Why not? It's bloody hot up there in the summer. And all the best dope comes from places with pretty extreme climates, up in mountain areas — Tibet, Nepal, Afghanistan, Colombia."

Albert said:—

"There's certainly a shortage at the moment. We could call it Colombian — nobody ever seems quite sure what Colombian looks like. Give me twenty-four hours to think about it, will you? It shouldn't be any problem at all."

Chapter XIX
GOODBYE ALBERT

Just in case Albert wasn't able to come up with anything Eddy spent the following morning trying to track down acquaintances in Notting Hill. Because of the day-long traffic congestion and the lack of parking spaces, he took the tube. (He was struck by all the unfamiliar adverts for familiar items in the underground stations.) When at last he returned to the hotel he found Barbro had gone out with the Aliens, taking the car.

"There was a phone call for her," the desk clerk told him. "They went out straightaway afterwards."

"Do you know who phoned?"

"It was a man."

"A foreigner?"

"English, I think. He asked for you first, then spoke to your wife."

Eddy thought this odd, but there was little he could do but sit in their room and wait. He felt depressed. He was already sick of London, its sleaziness and decay. And all those buildings, at first sight so excitingly various, had already by their profusion dulled his mind and paralysed his memory and had become infinitely more boring than the unending forests of Norrbotten. In order not to have to think about it he stretched out on one of the beds and tried to sleep. He was just beginning to doze off when the Aliens came in.

"*Vad gör du här?*" and "*Här är pappa*," they shrieked, simultaneously. Barbro, looking cross, followed them into the room.

"Where've you been?" Eddy asked. "Who phoned you?"

"Was it a joke?" Barbro seemed puzzled. She explained that Albert had phoned her, telling her to come to the church with the kids, to collect Eddy. When she reached the church, Albert had met her and explained that Eddy was waiting for them in a pub in Hampstead, having gone on ahead with another friend. He suggested Barbro should leave the Volvo, since he could drive her and the kids to Hampstead himself. This seemed perfectly reasonable; Barbro found London totally confusing and had taken nearly an hour to find the church. Leaving the Volvo at the church, therefore, Barbro and the kids got into Albert's Rover and they set out. Somewhere in Islington — at least that's where it sounded like from Barbro's account — Albert's car suddenly broke down. "It'll probably take me a good half hour to fix it," he said, and he hailed a taxi to take Barbro and the kids on to Hampstead. Eddy, he said, would be waiting for them in Jack Straw's Castle, at the top of the Heath. The taxi would take them right up to the front entrance. But when Barbro and the Aliens finally reached Jack Straw's Castle, there was no sign of Eddy. After waiting half an hour, Barbro decided to return to the hotel.

By the time Barbro had completed her account, Eddy had realized precisely what had happened.

He had been robbed.

He couldn't believe Albert could have done such a thing to him, but it was no good worrying about believing or not believing; he had just been diddled out of £10,000 worth of dope.

Albert must have noticed the steering-wheel lock he carried in the car, which would have been why he had set up the deliberate charade of the rendezvous at Jack Straw's Castle, instead of merely breaking into the Volvo outside the hotel and driving it away. It was merely chance that it had been Barbro who was the one to have been made a fool of. If he had been in the hotel when Albert had phoned, they would have tried some slightly different plan.

Trying to sound unperturbed, Eddy said:–

"I'd better get down to the church to get the car back."

He took a taxi to within a couple of blocks of the church. It was already growing dark when he arrived outside the wooden gates. They were closed, but he had no problem in scrambling over the adjoining wall. His Volvo was parked next to Albert's Jaquar in the yard. He opened the hatch-back. The carpet on the platform behind the back seat had been taken up and put back carelessly. It looked as if Albert had already laid his hands on the dope. And on the pistol Eddy had rashly hidden with it.

The door into the clergy house was open. Eddy stood inside the hall, listening for a moment, but he could hear nothing. There was a workshop just off the hall, with tools scattered on the benches and fixed on clips to the walls. Under one of the benches was a sledge-hammer. Eddy picked it up. There had been a time when he had fancied himself as a man who could break with his bare hands anything he could move, but finger bones get busted awfully easily in fist-fights, and it wasn't any fun touching up a woman with one's hands in plaster. Holding the sledge-hammer halfway along its handle he went upstairs.

The light was on in Albert's room. As quietly as he could Eddy leaned the sledge-hammer against the wall of the corridor, and pushed open Albert's door. Albert was sprawled in the elm captain's chair he had formerly had in his room in Camden Town. He looked up as Eddy came in. The conversation as far as Eddy remembered it later was more or less as follows:—

Albert said, genially:—

"Ah, at last, I've been waiting for you."

Eddy said, not so genially:—

"Looks like you've done a number on me."

Albert took the Husqvarna pistol from his pocket. He said:—

"I was going to have a couple of lads on hand in case you tried anything foolish, but then I found this in your car, so I sent the lads out to the pub over the road. No point involving too many other people in your problems. And I thought it'd be nicer if we were able to have a cosy little chat on our own."

Eddy said:—

"Let's chat, then."

Albert said:—

"Well, you know, in a way, I'm sorry about all this. Too much to expect that there shouldn't be too many hard feelings, I suppose?" But he couldn't help smirking. "You're welcome to the car back, of course. Always thought them a bit under-powered, Volvos."

"I'll want the dope back too."

"I've got the gun."

I've got the gun. It was odd how like the movies it was. *Stick 'em up or I'll blast you.*

"You wouldn't dare kill me."

"Possibly not. But a bullet in the knee is awful painful, and even with a bullet in the knee, I doubt if you'd care to complain to the Filth."

"But I need that dope."

"So do I. There's you, living like a ponce in Sweden, you don't know the problems we businessmen have. I need to raise thirty gees by next week. I'm some of the way. Your dope'll get me a lot of the rest."

"But what about me?"

"Like I said, we businessmen have problems. If other people have problems too, that's their look-out."

"So you just expect me to leave?"

"The sooner the better."

"Why are you doing this to me?" This was the first time in his life that Eddy understood how humiliated those old men must have felt in their dingy squalid rooms, when he had come to evict them.

Albert said:—

"You're just a hop-head. I saw it coming — how long ago was it? — seven, eight years ago. You could have been good, but you were getting soft. You've got to be careful with dope. Too much of it and it rots the brain. Not like booze; and it doesn't give early warnings either. No hangovers, no shakes, no D.T.s Too much dope and you might never notice there's a thing wrong with you, but little by little you lose your grip on things, till one fine day you wake up in the morning and discover you're a has-been. That's what's happened to you, Eddy."

Eddy stepped over to the door. Albert was still covering him with the pistol. Eddy said:—

"What right have you got to talk down to me like that?"

That's what he said, though it seemed pretty inadequate. But what can you say when the man you formerly admired more than any other man you every met — in reality, the only man you ever admired at all, in a whole lifetime of accepting people, even occasionally liking people, without ever once having a particularly high opinion of their qualities — the only person you ever loved, without even a wee bit of contempt — the man whom you thought the better of for having cheated, because remorse made you recollect how much you already owed to him even before you secretly robbed him — what can you say when this man blithely steals your last chance of making enough money to keep your home together and your kids clothed and fed, steals your notion of yourself as one of the rippers-off rather than one of the ripped-offs, steals any idea you had that you were the kind of guy friends remembered and were loyal to?

"Goodbye," he said.

Outside in the corridor he grabbed the sledge-hammer propped against the wall and sprinted up the short flight of stairs to the small arched doorway leading out on to the flat section of the roof.

It was now completely dark outside. The roof-top overlooked some warehouses along the far side of a street. The buildings in between had been demolished. There were a few street lights which cast a strange luminosity, as if under water, but no sign of any people. In the other direction the red warning beacon on top of the still incomplete National Westminster Building glared malevolently, like a contemptuous watching eye.

Albert reached the doorway behind him, gun in hand.

"You're a loony," he shouted. "Are you going to stay out there all night? There'll be a couple of my lads along later on. You don't want your arms and legs broken along with everything else, do you?" By way of answer, Eddy, who had scrambled up the side of the dormer in which the door was set till he reached the chimney stack at the end of the building, toppled one of the chimney pots into the yard below.

"You cunt," said Albert.

The flat part of the roof was quite small, over-shadowed by higher pitched sections, the lower parts of which were skirted by a parapet that went all round the top of the building. In order to get a better view of Eddy, Albert began edging along the narrow space between one of these pitched sections and the parapet. Between the parapet and the pitched roof there was a rain gutter. Albert contrived to get his foot stuck in it, and had to bend down to free himself.

Albert was just straightening up when Eddy launched himself down the side of the roof, slithering bump-bump-bump over the slates, and dropped to his feet right beside him. Eddy had neither time nor space to swing the sledge-hammer properly, but he caught Albert with it full on the side of the throat just below the ear, and there was enough force in the blow to make Eddy's hands tingle.

Albert went over the parapet. It was a drop of about thirty feet to the yard below. You were likely to break an arm or leg if you fell that far, shake yourself up badly, but you wouldn't actually kill yourself unless you were very unlucky.

Albert was very unlucky. He was dead before he hit the ground.

Eddy wiped the handle of the sledge-hammer and replaced it in the workshop on his way outside. The pistol lay beside Albert's body.

He tucked it in his waistband and went through Albert's pockets. There was only £34 in Albert's wallet. Eddy left it and took only Albert's keys. He felt as if he was in a trance. He had forgotten how awfully *physical* violence was.

When he opened the safe in Albert's office, he found an unexpected bonus. Albert had mentioned that he was scraping together money for something big. There was nearly £10,000 there, along with Eddy's dope.

Eddy examined the dope. He had wrapped it in polythene bags of West German manufacture. They seemed to have no serial numbers. There was nothing to connect the dope with Sweden. He decided to leave it. If anyone, on learning of Albert's demise, enquired after the money in his safe, they would have an answer of sorts. Possibly a very inconvenient answer, if the police were in on the case. He loaded the money in a plastic carrier bag and returned the keys to Albert's pocket.

He had a good look at the man he had killed, because of course he was going to have to remember every detail for the rest of his life. His former boss lay unsymmetrically spread-eagled in a corner of the yard that was strewn with the rubbish which had always seemed inseparable from his life: bricks, lengths of four-by-four beams, an old bucket, a partly stripped-down engine, a broken lavatory seat, bits of the chimney pot Eddy had thrown down. His face was cut but not bleeding. The amount of rubbish he had fallen on, he could easily have broken his neck, easily have bruised himself on the side of the throat.

Anyway, how else were they going to explain the injury he had died of? A blow from a sledge-hammer might have done it, but after all, what kind of *animal* would hit an unarmed man with a sledgehammer?

Chapter XX
END

A few evenings later.

They had sold the car at Göteborg; instead of two days of solid driving Eddy wanted to be free to sit back in a railway carriage and readjust to his adopted country.

As the train rumbled and creaked through the long melancholy twilight, passing level-crossings with their doleful bells every twenty minutes or so, the sense of Sweden grew on him. Gävle, a glimpse of right-angled streets and, on the other side of the tracks from the station building, a church like a smallish Zeppelin hanger which, in another world, another life, he might have sold the pews from, they reached just as the great lamps along the platform came on. By Sundsvall it was quite dark. Between Hällnas and Åsträsk the train stopped for ten minutes in the middle of nowhere, just dense silent forest crowding in on each side beyond the wire fencing parallel to the railway line. He wanted to get down from the carriage and lose himself amongst those Swedish trees. He even opened the outer door, acting casual as if merely wishing to look down the length of the train to see why they had stopped, but he closed it again when Barbro came out of their sleeping compartment in her dressing gown.

"So we're home," he said. According to the timetable they should have been in Basuträsk five minutes ago. Eddy thought of that idea he had once had of Sweden as a totalitarian state devoted to precision efficiency and split-second punctuality — a kind of super-Italy-under-Mussolini — which had somehow gone soft from too many decades of success. Or was it just that the summers were so short that they never readjusted from the annual trauma of the great winter snows?

"How did you like your holiday?"

"I would have liked to have gone to the theatre. To see a play by Agatha Christie."

"That's just for foreign tourists."

"I was a foreign tourist."

Perhaps, he thought, everyone goes through life as a foreign tourist. Yet he didn't really believe that. Ever since their return from London he had had a tremendously strong sense of belonging. His own native country might be going down the drain, but he had faith that the human race was going somewhere interesting. He had glimpsed that future because he was living where a more advanced and better organized civilization survived on a knife edge in almost extra-terrestrial conditions. He had returned for one last look at his past. He had enjoyed their visit to London, had been stimulated by it almost as if it was a drug he had been searching for. But now that he was back in Sweden, he knew that London was a phase in his life that was completely over. He now belonged in Sweden. As far as he was concerned, the collapse of the British social and political system, which was coming sooner or later, would be just another front page story in *Dagens Nyheter*.

He tried to explain this to Barbro.

"Oh boy, you're strange;" she said. It had been years since she had last said that to him.

But Eddy didn't think he was strange at all. He thought of himself as the prototype twenty-first century man.

CPSIA information can be obtained
at www.ICGtesting.com
Printed in the USA
FFOW04n1256260515
13591FF